ADAM HALL

Queen In Danger

HarperPaperbacks
A Division of HarperCollins*Publishers*

HarperPaperbacks *A Division of* HarperCollins*Publishers*
10 East 53rd Street, New York, N.Y. 10022

This book is published by arrangement with the author.

Cover photography by Herman Estevez

First HarperPaperbacks printing: December 1990

Printed in the United States of America

HarperPaperbacks and colophon are trademarks of
HarperCollins*Publishers*

10 9 8 7 6 5 4 3 2

To June and Philip

1st

MOVE

FEAR HAD not yet entered the mind of the woman in green. She would be free of it for another five minutes; perhaps six—but no more than six, because, she was walking quickly, along a pathway in St. James's Park.

Spring had come to London, possibly from Paris overnight and travelling light, to drape green gossamer among the skeletonic twigs and blow a zephyr's breath against the Royal Standard, high above Buckingham Palace. The Queen was at home. Under the plane-trees of the parks burned the candle-flames of crocuses, amethyst and ocher and already opening to the morning sun.

Along the pavement of Piccadilly went the

Right Reverend Bishop Pimblett (or "Pimples" to his niece), and as he turned towards the Athenaeum Club a man who swung fifty feet above him on a builder's cradle dropped a brush by accident, and swore. Charles Herbert Smith (or "Charlie-boy" to his mates) looked down, and saw his brush miss the bishop by a bristle's length, and somehow felt disappointed.

From the Circus to Hyde Park Corner the great red buses went, a moving comic-strip of advertising posters; and taxis fretted at the traffic lights, flags up, flags down, get on wiv it, can't you—we 'aven't got all day. It was spring, and London was doing all right. Papers were up a ha'penny and fares'd go up again next; but the sun were well up too, and the Queen was in, and just look at them lovely crocuses—no good grumbling, is it, eh?

Two Jamaican airmen crossed the road near Berkeley Street, boots and buttons polished up like glass; and there was the woman in green again, a little way behind them. She stopped to buy a paper, then walked on, folding it and tucking it beneath her arm. From his cabin a bus-driver looked at her, because she was young and walked with a neat, quick step in her olive-green tailored suit. Just the job, he thought, and heard the ping of his bell like a prick of conscience, because Millie looked a treat, too, specially Saturdays.

The woman in green turned into Bond Street,

and her shadow was killed, suddenly and silently by the high corner buildings, but her reflection went beside her across the shop-windows, changing her for an instant into a Hartnell gown, decking her now with a diamond clip at seven hundred pounds. Two women passed her, with plain plump overbred Mayfair faces and very exquisite shoes. A taxi drew in to the curb, the rear door already opening because in London time is always short.

She moved—represented by her glassy sister—in a florist's window-pane, stepping through a frenzy of mimosa, plucking none but passing on, nearing the first bombed-site, now without shadow and without reflection; and still, for a few last moments, without fear.

She had passed through many doors today, but now, as she went into the *Salon des Fleurs*, she opened the last door that held her back from the sudden fear that had come to meet her here, among the flower-bowls, amid the perfumed air.

The heavy glass swung behind her, and the click of her heels over the parquet was sharp and intimate, shut away from the street.

Marette, pencil poised behind the reception desk, tried not to shout at Mrs. Carmody. Mrs. Carmody adjusted her little black deaf-aid and leaned her thirteen stone against the desk. She caught a word or two, and nodded, beaming.

"*Three* o'clock, yes, yes—*three* o'clock, *quite*."

Marette relaxed, her pencil jerking over the page.

The woman in green stood waiting, unfolding the newspaper she had bought and holding it flat.

Mrs. Carmody said in a low, hooting tone: "Mr. Edouard *personally*." Marette nodded, giving a brilliant smile.

"Of course, Mrs. Carmody."

"What?"

"Of course—*per*sonally."

Mrs. Carmody gave a vigorous nod and turned for the doors, with the deliberation of an infantryman upon maneuvers, her powerful handbag prepared to shoot from the hip.

Marette drew a slight breath of relief, and looked at the woman in green.

"So sorry to have kept you waiting, Mrs. Tasman."

Mrs. Carmody forced an exit, and now silence crept in, its tail almost caught in the doors as their heavy glass swung shut.

The woman in green looked up from the newspaper, and stared at Marette; and Marette felt a sudden chill along her nerves, for she was exposed to a stare that did not see her, a stare of eyes in which there was no recognition. Mrs. Tasman, looking straight at the receptionist, saw someone else, someone who was not in here. Then the wide hazel eyes changed, and saw

Marette in her light blue smock, standing behind the desk.

Mrs. Tasman spoke softly, as if waked from a drugged sleep.

"I ... came in"—her small gloved hand brushed across her brow, trying to contact memory of normal things by physical touch—"to make an appointment."

Marette looked away from the strange, bewildered eyes, and held her pencil ready.

"Yes, Mrs. Tasman."

The woman in green folded the newspaper, forcing herself to go on as the color crept back to her face:

"For ... tomorrow. Can you fit me in after lunch?"

The pencil skated without touching, and found a space.

"Would four o'clock be convenient?"

The noon edition was folded, again and then again, folded tightly into a soft white stick.

"If I can leave by five."

Softly Marette said: "Is it just for a face-pack, Mrs. Tasman?" Her voice was soothing, and led the woman gently back, gently to the normal, ordinary day, here where the light was warm and the flower-bowls calm with blooms. Behind her and beyond the windows, the street ran by like a silent film, not reaching the stillness here.

"Just a face-pack, yes, Marette."

"You should be away by five, then."

"Thank you."

Mrs. Tasman turned away, and met the ghost of her reflection in the door. When she opened it, and went into the street, the soft white stick was in the wastepaper basket near the desk, slowly unfolding, moment by moment, as if it had life of its own.

The Miller-Group building took up four acres of Fleet Street and stood eight stories high, square-built and bare-faced opposite its major rival, the Criterion Press.

Miller-Group put out six publications a week, three a month and one half-yearly. Content ranged from the smarty strips of *Kine-Comic* to the oh-so-candid-camera shots of huntball guests in *The Squire*, with a range of readership from young Snotty Higgins in Tooting to Lady Amelia Truscott in Park Lane.

Editor-in-Chief Maurice Jerrold sat in his first floor office, and tilted his half handredweight of period chair, and looked at *Venus*. He held one of the first dozen copies, the rest of its two hundred thousand circulation would clear the presses by this evening, and tomorrow morning *Venus* would reach Cardiff, and Manchester, and York.

Jerrold frisked the pages, smelling the sour-sweet bouquet of the virgin paper. Three-color cover: close-up of tiger-lily with artificial dew—

editorial by Maurice Jerrold (Spring is How You Greet It)—Beauty-Box gossip by Enid Cavendish (All Hands A-deck) with an off-the-record rake-off from Luxor Jewels Limited—center-spread by Gloria del Ray (Body-line Bowing—top secret previews of the new Paris collections)—and a brief dignified postscript to the editorial: "Owing to the recent increase in the price of paper, etc. . . . in company with other leading periodicals, etc. . . . Venus will now cost Three Shillings."

Jerrold reached the rear advertisements and stopped worrying about the artificial dew on the tiger-lily that looked more like heavy rain, and the center-spread title that somehow didn't seem to hit it quite; because nothing could stop the torrent of the two hundred thousand now the flood-gates were down. These criticisms apart, *Venus* looked all right: normal dreadful, or nine out of ten. Jerrold was his own cruellest critic, which was why *Venus* led the top three women's glossies by a well-groomed head.

One of the ivory telephones rang, and Jerrold picked it up.

"Yes?"

"Salmson's have a strike on, Mr. Jerrold, in their Birmingham area—"

"How many copies?"

"Seventeen thousand."

"Let Bradley handle them. Phone him now."

"Yes, Mr. Jerrold."

"Three per cent plus. Has Mrs. Tasman come in?"

"Yes, a minute ago—"

"I'd like to see her."

"I'll tell her, Mr. Jerrold."

He cradled the telephone and leaned his big arms on the desk, and gazed at the tiger-lily. Spring sunshine sent a bright sheen across the varnished paper, so that the darker hues became dazzling, leaving the light tones matt; and the lily lost its flamboyant personality and admitted artifice; it was a mere two-dimensional total of colors, a summing-up of design, flat, painted and false.

Before the door opened, Jerrold slid the noon edition of the *Standard* into a desk-drawer, and leaned back, tilting his chair again. He said:

"Well?"

Thelma closed the door, moving to the desk and looking down at *Venus*.

"I feel I've let you down."

"Why?"

"My title. It looks worse than I'd dreamed."

"It's a little contrived. That's all."

She turned away, taking a cigarette from the box on the cabinet, looking at the big photograph of Jerrold with Laura and their two children. She lit the cigarette and said: "What I hate is that if anyone else had pushed in a title like that you'd have cut out their heart."

He shrugged, getting up.

"If anyone else had pushed it in, it would have been good—for them. When you set yourself a high standard, sometimes your arm aches. Next week's another day. Will you come and have lunch, Thelma?"

He watched her carefully, and thought that she knew, had seen the noon edition of the *Standard*. Her eyes were nervy and she was smoking too quickly, and she was worried about the Body-line Bowing title more than she ought to be. It wasn't that bad.

"Thanks Maurice, but I—"

She started and her eyes widened as a telephone bell cut in. He picked up the receiver.

"Yes?"

"Bradley's going ahead now, Mr. Jerrold."

"Good. Wire an emergency contract."

"Plus three."

"That's right."

"Very good, Mr. Jerrold."

He dropped the telephone and said:

"But you're lunching with Victor."

She turned from the big photograph, where the two boys gazed at the camera, rather plump and rather aggressive in a good-humored what-the-hell kind of way, and very serious about life, very like Maurice.

She said: "Yes. He's leaving just afterwards, going to Bristol to sell a supercharger or something—"

He stood behind her and slightly to one side,

his big hands dug into his pockets.

"With Vic away, you're going to be lonely. Come and stay with us for a week—"

"That's nice of you, but I'll manage."

"Laura would like it. I'll phone her now."

She put a hand on his arm, her eyes grateful, but still with the fear behind them. He was a big solid man, the epitome of the Miller-Group building itself; and she knew that in a real emergency she could rely on him. That was a lot to know, and to believe in; but the emergency was not yet real; it was only, so far, amorphous, a shaggy and prowling threat.

"No, Maurice, please. Laura and I get on well; and I don't want to spoil a nice relationship. She doesn't want your protégée eating out of her ration books for a whole week, and—"

"Then bring yours. And stop thinking of yourself as my protégée." He moved away from her a little, looking through the enormous window, down into the street. "I made you into a fashion writer and showed you the ropes. You've paid me back and we're quits. You needn't picture yourself as a little lost orphan of the storm taking shelter in this paper palace of mine. You're good and you're tough and you're part of the outfit. Circulation's gone up three per cent since you joined us. That isn't much—but it should have dropped twenty over the same period because of the paper cut: most of the others have. Maybe it's my editorials, or Willison's photographs. I think it's the Gloria del Ray center-spread. If it isn't, you're the best fashion-talker we've had since the war."

His flecked brown eyes looked across to the Criterion building, and did not see it, huge though it was against the sky. He just saw the sub-headline in the noon edition, and hoped things would be all right. His head turned a fraction and he grinned.

"But don't ask for a raise; we've got a price-crisis on."

She was moving to the door, her shoes silent over the heavy pile. She looked back at him, and he saw the effort behind her smile, and the small nervous tension of her gloved hands.

"I won't, Maurice."

He turned and, without wanting to, said one word more that would tell her he'd seen the sub-headline and wanted to protect her if the need came.

"Thelma, let's phone Laura. She'd love to have you with us for a week—"

"I appreciate it, very much. And I'd love to do it. But some other time, as a holiday, not an escape."

For an instant in the sunshine they looked straight at each other; then she opened the door, calling back:

"Give Laura my love. And a slap on the bottom for Mick and Jonathan from Aunt Thelma."

"All right, then."

When she left the office, he stood for a little while at the window, looking down again into the street; and for the first time since he had seen the newspaper he found himself watching the man down there who was getting out of a taxi, and the other one who was crossing the street towards this pavement, and the third man who stood at the corner by the bookshop, smoking a cigarette.

He knew that Thelma would be watching them, too, and others like them, all of them innocent men, all of them strangers, unless ... suddenly among them there came the particular one, the man in the noon edition.

Thelma looked in at her own office again before she left for lunch. Marjorie was working on, making up in advance for an early knock-off this afternoon; Friday night was Amami night, and tomorrow there was Brighton. Marjorie looked like a sparrow and talked always with a slight nervous flutter, her words falling like rejected crumbs.

"Weird personage phoned."

Thelma tugged at the drawer of her desk and checked her commitments sheet for the rest of the day. She murmured:

"What sort of weird personage?"

She looked at the sheet and read *Three o'clock —drink with Anton Pomery, talk about hats. (Has he bought space?)*

"Didn't give his name," Marjorie said.

Four-fifteen—dress-show at Hannerby's—take Rex.

"Wanted to talk to a Mrs. Speight," Marjorie said.

Five-thirty—cocktail party at—

Thelma looked at Marjorie.

"What did you say?"

"He wanted a Mrs. Speight. Told him not known here. He said she was beauty editor. I said ours was G. del R." Marjorie began captioning some photographs from America. Thelma looked down at her commitments sheet again, feeling suddenly chilled, and weak, and helpless. Her scalp was creeping, as if the appointments on the list were execution dates that she must cover for her magazine.

Marjorie said: "I told him G. del R. was a Mrs. Tasman, to make it clear we knew no Speight. He said 'Oh,' as if I was lying. Also Pomery phoned—would you make it three-fifteen, he's rushed?"

Thelma opened her fountain-pen.

She asked: "Did he say anything else?"

"Apologized."

"No, the man who wanted to—"

"Oh. Don't think so. He rang off."

Thelma corrected the three-o'clock appointment to read three-fifteen, and closed her pen, screwing the cap slowly home. Marjorie said:

"Why?"

"No reason," Thelma said. She shut the drawer, picked up her bag and moved to the door. Marjorie looked up from her photographs and said:

"I'll be gone by five."

Thelma turned, and looked at her, and for a moment Marjorie had the strange feeling that she was being looked clean through, as if she were glass. Then Thelma said:

"All right, I'll get the key from the night desk."

She went out, and just before the door closed Marjorie called "Have a nice week-end," but all she heard were the high-heeled footsteps going down the passage. For a few seconds, before she hit the keys of her Remington, she gazed at the door panels and wished she didn't have a short, plump body like a bird's but one like Thelma's instead, and a center-spread commission, and a pseudonym like Gloria del Ray.

Then she looked at the news-photograph on the top of the pile, and banged out a caption on the typewriter. *For the whippet-hipped . . . a sleek inspiration from New York in the best Lincoln Highway going-my-way manner. . . .*

The keys chattered out their trivial gossip. The model in the photograph grinned up at the typist, whippet-hipped and dentally exposed. You can't have everything. You don't even want it, if you're wise.

2nd

MOVE

YELLOW TULIPS were there, seven in a bowl, bright as agony in the sunshine. It was almost astonishing that color so brilliant should cast a shadow no more than mere grey on the tablecloth; but there on the tablecloth were the seven gray heads.

Beyond the window a Daimler glided by, its American-style white-walled tires rolling with a calm grandiloquence along the street. A bus lunged after it, boisterous and advertisement-garlanded and busy with its lot. From in here, the seven yellow chalices appeared to grow in a woodland dell of glass and masonry, paving-stones and motor cars, with somewhere a tinny car horn piping like a bird.

At the end of the restaurant the doors swung shut; the head-waiter moved, an alerted penguin, dapper and polite. He brought them to the table, and for a moment the tulips grew against a background of her moss green dress. She looked up at Victor, with a quick appeal in her clouded hazel eyes.

"Could we—have another table? Not by the window?"

He seemed surprised; tall, sleek-haired and well groomed, unlike an enthusiastic engineer, he gave a shrug.

"I thought you liked the sunshine—"

"Yes, but—it's a little bright, today. Do you mind?"

Past the long window a man walked, glancing in, then walking on. She watched him with one swift glance and looked away.

Tasman spoke to the waiter. There was another table, unreserved. He took them there. It was in a corner, at the far end from the doors. From here she could see everyone who came in.

Tasman quizzed her when they had sat down.

"All right?"

"Yes, I'm sorry, darling. Late night last night. Spring's a searching season for a woman's face."

He smiled. "Paragraph. We must remember, too, that in this season much can be done about scientific dieting, for skin and general health. Period."

"Pig."

"I can't give you a greater compliment, quoting from Gloria del Ray."

"Not in that tone of voice. I'm going to learn to mimic a supercharger."

"If you do, your escort'll be arrested, because they scream. What are you edgy about today?"

"I'm not."

"Something private, obviously."

"I'm just not edgy. Shall we have salad?"

"Of course. For skin and general health—"

"Please don't labor it."

He glanced up from the menu, then down again.

"Sorry."

She touched his hand.

"Maybe I am on edge, but there's no reason. A week away from me should do you good."

"Wish you could come with me."

"I've more shows to cover during the next week than I've had in the past month. It's spring, and the *salons* are bustin' out all over." She studied his lean, rather lopsided face, and some of the constant fear went from her eyes, and tenderness was there. "You *will* only be away for a week, Victor?"

He was pleased, and reassured, believing from her tone that she would miss him when he went; and he was not entirely wrong. She would miss him, as well as his protection.

"Yes, of course. Back next Friday. Meet me at the station with a cab and we'll do a show, a sup-

per, and finish up at Jack and Daphne Baker's."
He ticked off the items on his fingers, and she
nodded with a smile.

"Bless you, it's a date. Maurice was nice this
morning. I told him you were going and he
wanted to ring Laura and say I'd stay with them
for a week."

"Going to?"

"No. I didn't want to impose on her. It must
be tricky running a home for an editor-in-chief,
without his staff, We'd only talk shop till she
screamed."

"But it was nice of him. I like to think you're
with him, while I'm away. He's too much in love
with his wife to want to seduce you, but fond
enough of you to look after you."

"He's too nice to seduce me, anyway."

"The nicest types fall for your looks. I'm just
the exception." He looked at her seriously for an
instant. "Wish we could marry, Thelma."

She looked away.

"We've been over all that, darling. Sorry I'm
obstinate, but—I suppose it's just a feeling."

"Something to do with surrendering personal
sovereignty—Career-women Must be Free—"

"That sounds pretty horrid, but if it were better
put it might be somewhere near the truth."

He said nothing, dismissing the thought. She
said: "Vic, I couldn't love you more, and I'd like
to be with you all my life. Will that do?"

Their hands touched, then drew away as the

waiter came. Victor nodded to her, across the waiter's ministering hands.

The big man bought a paper in Ludgate Hill, giving the newsvendor a penny.

"Livin' in the past?" the news vendor said, the penny still on his opened hand.

"What?"

"Three-'a'pence, these days, chum."

"Oh."

The big man gave him another halfpenny and walked away, opening the paper as he went. His feet dragged a little, as if he were tired, or perhaps did not care. His hat was shapeless and his suit did not fit him. When he reached the last bombed site before the bridge, he looked up and turned his head, and moved towards the barrier at the pavement's edge. He leaned on its timbers, gazing down into the area of flattened masonry, where grass and weeds grew, green and kindly over the bric-â-brac. After a while he took a worn pencil-stub from his pocket, and made a sketch on the edge of the newspaper, looking many times at the bombed-site; but his sketch was of a man, and there was no man there.

Ten minutes passed, and he put the pencil-stub away, folding the paper and walking on. His gait said that he had achieved nothing, but would try again. In the way his head was held, and in the way he walked, there was expressed a patience that was more than natural.

He came to Fleet Street, and walked until he was opposite the Miller-Group building. Here he paused, and stood on the edge of the pavement, looking up at the building, at each window, at each story, at every person who went through the great main doors, or came into the street. Then he moved again with his dragging, patient feet, and through a dozen side lanes reached a shabby road, and went into a house, and up the stairs.

In his room was a bed, and little more. There were no clothes on the hooks behind the door, and no shoes anywhere, nor a single suit-case. This was a room not to live in, but to be lonely in, or brood, or sleep, or wait. He sat on the edge of the bed, his big frame curved as he leaned his arms on his knees and stared at the dingy wall.

Somewhere below him in the house a clock chimed; and later a kid shouted to another in the road outside; and later still a cistern flushed with a muffled, distant gasp. For a long time he sat and looked at the wall, and through the wall to the last bombed site before the bridge, and the Miller-Group building farther on. Then he turned and lay on the bed, facing the small square window, and looked at the patch of sky.

The bright blue was reflected in his eyes, and in his eyes there was calm, horrible patience. Although alone, he was not lonely here; nor was he here to brood. Although on the bed, he did not want to sleep. He had come to wait; and as he stared at the sky, and saw the shadows mounting on the rooftops opposite, it would have been clear to see—had any been here to see—that he was waiting for one thing only, and that was the night.

3rd

MOVE

BISHOP TOOK a pipe-cleaner and pushed it through the stem of his meerschaum; then he worked on the shank.

"That sort of thing should be done in the bathroom," Miss Gorringe said.

Bishop dropped the pipe-cleaner into the ash bowl, fitted the amber stem with affectionate care, looked at Miss Gorringe and said:

"You'd never get the pipe-cleaner down the plug hole. And in any case, love me, love my pipe."

"I think you're both insanitary. Can we talk business?"

"It might be less personal."

Vera Gorringe picked up two files from the

end of Bishop's desk, took them with her to the davenport, and sat down.

"These files have been on your desk since the lunch-time edition of the *Evening Standard* was on the street. Don't you want some work?"

He sent her an oblique glance.

"It means work?"

"It might. You shall judge."

He perched on the end of the heavy desk, and began filling his pipe. Miss Gorringe opened the top file.

"Speight is free," she said.

"Who?"

"Capital ess pee ee i gee aitch tee. Mervyn Speight, found guilty but insane two years ago at the Central Criminal Court and committed to Broadmoor Asylum."

Bishop struck a match.

He said: "For a murder?"

"Yes. Victim was a woman called Joanna Martin—"

"Found dead on a bombed-site in Ludgate Hill. Right?"

"Yes. Nothing wrong with your memory, Hugo."

"It's selective. I don't see this means a job for me."

"You may. An escaped homicidal maniac isn't the least interesting person in the world. You ought to have a talk with him."

Bishop watched her steadily. Trust Gorry to be on to something like this, within twelve hours of the event. He remembered a year ago, when she had come into this room and slapped a cablegram on his desk: *Woman's lacquered fingernails found in stomach of dead shark off Teneriffe. Interest Bishop?* A month afterwards a ship's steward was arrested in Cape Town, and Bishop came back to file the facts in his casebook: a murder had lost perfection because the shark had kept the evidence; but Gorry had found him the job. Middle-aged and conservative, with a taste for embroidery and an Oxford degree, Vera Gorringe had also a flair for nosing out the fantastic, the incredible and the macabre. An insane murderer had just escaped: she thought Bishop should have a talk with him. That was Gorry.

"You know where he is?"

She shook her head.

"No. But we could find him."

"How?"

"If you can't, who can? Try his wife first; I'll give you her address."

Bishop got off the desk and began walking the length of the room.

"His wife—" he said quietly.

From the davenport, Miss Gorringe glanced up.

She said: "I thought that would make a connection. If you want a new case for your *Personality Under Stress,* it might be the wife who'd provide it, better than the maniac. Shall I tell you about her?"

"Do."

"Mrs Thelma Speight had been married for three years before her husband was put on trial. She'd met him at an art school. By the time he was sent to Broadmoor he'd become something of a professional painter, with something of a reputation. Very soon after the trial, she left England and lived alone in Italy to escape the aftermath of notoriety—"

"Did she attend the trial?"

"Yes, she was loyal throughout." Miss Gorringe turned a page of the second file. "Despite the fact that, as far as I can find out, the marriage wasn't happy. He had too much temperament and she didn't know which way to handle it."

"Where did you get this behind-the-scenes picture of a marriage that began five years ago?"

Miss Gorringe concentrated on her notes.

"Learn the language of the sparrows. They sit on every window-sill. Last year, Thelma Speight arrived back in England as Mrs Thelma Tasman. With her came Victor Tasman, technical representative of a British-owned aircraft and allied products company—"

"They'd married, abroad?"

"They couldn't. She has never divorced her husband. But as far as the world is concerned, Mr and Mrs Victor Tasman are man and wife."

Bishop stopped pacing, and stood over Miss Gorringe, his long head tilted to look at the files. This dislodged the first flakes of ash from his pipe, and they fell delicately on to her papers.

She observed them.

"This room is twenty feet long and sixteen feet wide. It has nine chairs and two desks and a good half-dozen ashtrays. Must I say more?"

"No, but you probably will."

He turned away, mooching thoughtfully across to his desk in the bay window. Sitting behind it, he heard faintly the murmur of traffic along King's Road, and, cutting across it, Gorry's voice:

"Thelma Tasman kept away from the friends she had known; but one man—who had offered his assistance during the trial—saw her when she came back to England, and fixed her up with a job. He's Maurice Jerrold, editor-in-chief of the Miller-Group publishing house. Fifty, successful, happily married, two fine boys. Mrs Tasman now writes for two of his magazines under the pseudonym Gloria del Ray. I've read her stuff: it's first-rate."

"Why did Jerrold do this?"

"I can only guess that he was partly sorry for her and partly sensed that she had the makings of a fashion-writer for his magazine. If he did, he was right."

Bishop said: "What's their relationship?"

"You've a nasty mind—"

"You misconstrue me—"

"Since Jerrold is happily married with a nice home background, and Thelma is living with an up-and-coming young engineer, I think we can say that the Jerrold-Thelma relationship is that of chief editor and star fashion-writer plus mutual friendship."

Bishop sat hunched in his chair, gazing at the jade figure of a water-carrier on the desk. After a full minute he lifted his eyes and looked at Miss Gorringe. She sat neatly on the davenport, with her Raymonde-groomed blue-rinsed hair framed against the background of Regency-stripe curtains. Bishop said:

"You look a million dollars, babe."

She stiffened.

"Oh, *really*, Hugo! Please concentrate on escaped maniacs for the moment. And if you wish to compliment me, kindly remember I'm old enough to be your great-aunt, and choose a phrase more suitable."

"Yes, ma'am."

"Have you nothing sensible to say about the Speight affair?"

"Nothing."

She got up with a slight sigh, returning the files to the cabinet.

"Does it interest you?"

He said: "I don't know yet."

She turned towards the door at the end of the room. "Well, if you decide it does, the files are in there."

She opened the door, leaving him to think alone. Before it closed, the Princess Chu Yi-Hsin slipped in, and padded silently across the room, the light from the windows glinting in the great blue eyes.

Bishop turned his head as he caught the flash of smoky fur; the Siamese leapt and sat on her haunches near him on the desk, tail curled neatly around the chocolate feet, small head tilted to look at Bishop.

"Hello, Gorgeous," he said softly.

In the long room there was silence; the only movement was the faint curl of smoke lifting from the meerschaum bowl. For moment on moment the cat watched the smoke with a quiet, idle fascination; then Bishop slid open one of the heavy drawers, and there came the dull musical touching of ivory against ivory as he chose the *white Queen* from among the chess-pieces, and stood it on the desk.

The Siamese looked at it, perhaps seeing it as a white object of a certain height and shape, or as a tiny, pale, lifeless woman-animal, the same as the human who had left this room a while ago, but different, and small, and voiceless. The cat heard the man say:

"Thelma Speight, alias Thelma Tasman, alias Gloria del Ray: the Queen in danger."

His hand selected another chess-man from the drawer, and stood it—a *white Rook* —near the Queen.

"Maurice Jerrold: the Protector."

Chu Yi-Hsin moved her soft fawn head, watching the man who murmured. At an equal distance from the Queen he stood a *white Knight*.

"Victor Tasman, the Constant Lover."

For a moment he considered then behind the Queen—directly behind but at a greater distance—he put the *red King*.

"Mervyn Speight . . . husband, murderer and madman, enrobed in blood."

Beside the King he laid a *red Pawn*.

"Joanna Martin, dead by the King's hand, and bloodied too. . . ."

His long fingers toyed with the fifth piece for nearly a minute, while the cat watched, and the skein of smoke crept from the pipe's bowl upwards. The fifth piece was a *white* Bishop, and now he stood it on the desk, away from the others but facing them.

"My own namesake . . . quite at a standstill, and wondering where to begin."

 4th
MOVE

 THE TWO men walked, the lean one and the one with the dark blue suit, out of New Scotland Yard and along Whitehall. In Trafalgar Square the fountains still played, though it was evening, and the rising, falling water-plumes were tinted by the neon lights that blazed against Grand Buildings.

"So you haven't found him," Bishop said.

Detective-Inspector Frisnay said nothing. They went into a milk-bar, at the bottom of Charing Cross Road, and were perched on stools before Bishop spoke again.

"I think you *ought* to find him, Freddie. I mean, the bloke might go and pop someone off, just to celebrate his being on the loose. Then where would you be?"

"Anywhere," Frisnay said, "would be preferable to here, sitting with you, looking at milk. What d'you want?"

"Ham sandwich, as it'll come out of your expenses."

"I'm off duty."

"I hate to contradict you, but we're going to talk business."

"Whose?"

"Yours."

"D'you ever talk about your own?"

"It'd bore people. Besides, I haven't one. And a strawberry milk shake, please."

Frisnay screwed up his face.

"You asked for it. You can have it if you don't talk about Speight. I've had enough of him for one day."

He ordered two ham sandwiches, a strawberry milkshake and a milk-and-soda. Bishop said:

"Where are you looking for him?"

"Who?"

"Speight."

"No statement."

"All right, we won't talk about Speight. We'll talk about Mrs. Speight."

Frisnay watched the milk shakes being whisked, and wondered what all this electricity and chromium and chemical flavoring had to do with a simple rustic cow.

He said: "She's out of town."

Bishop looked at his milk-shake and had a vague feeling that Freddie was right about these things. They should have gone to a good old timber-built worm-eaten honest-to-God pub.

"Have your men called at her address?"

"Of course."

"What address?"

"Stapleton Crescent."

Bishop looked at him.

"But she doesn't live in Stapleton Crescent."

Frisnay shrugged, starting on his ham.

"That's the address they have at Broadmoor. It's where Speight sends his letters to her."

"Have you tried to phone her there?"

"We have."

"No answer?"

Bishop said: "Is her name in the directory?"

"No."

"You got the number from the authorities at Broadmoor?"

Frisnay nodded.

Bishop looked at the big chromium shake-whisk and saw his face reflected on its long round casing. His face looked like a humanized banana.

"I'm interested in Speight," he said.

Frisnay turned his slow brown eyes on Bishop.

"You surprise me."

Bishop said: "I think the address your men called on is the wrong one. A girl named Eve

Jordan lives at 19 Stapleton Crescent—was it 19 Stapleton Crescent?"

"Yes," Frisnay said, eyeing him steadily.

"And this girl, Eve Jordan, redirected the letters from Speight to his wife. Eve's a friend of hers, and . . . " his voice trailed off, and he lifted his milk-shake, gazing abstractedly into the pink froth. Frisnay waited, not going on with his sandwich, looking at Bishop like a visionary limpet.

Bishop drank up, and looked at the glass again, contemplatively.

"I should think," he said vaguely, "that you could almost shave with this stuff. I should think you could get quite a lather. Would you think so, Freddie?"

Frisnay said: "Is that just guesswork?"

"Well, naturally. Before you can be certain of anything, you have to try it—put it to the test. Now, if I had my shaving-brush with me, I could dip it in the froth and whop it on my—"

"About Eve Jordan," Frisnay said patiently. "Is it guesswork?"

"Eve who?" Bishop said, looking at him gently.

Frisnay said: "All right, Bishop. The point's made. I didn't want to talk about Speight; and now I do. Are you satisfied?"

Bishop looked at his watch.

"Forgive me, Frederick, but time presses. Life is very earnest, brother." He got off the stool.

Frisnay said: "You've had a nice big ham sandwich. Just tell me if you know the *right* address."

Bishop wandered amiably to the door.

"I happen to be going that way now. Why not come along?"

Frisnay caught up with him.

He said: "I think I will."

The lean man nodded to the one in the dark blue suit as they came out of the milk-bar in Charing Cross Road, and he said:

"Yes, I thought you would."

"Have we time?"

Rex said. "Of course. Sherry?"

She nodded, looking round the crowded ante-room. In the main *salon,* through the lofty doors, most of the seats were taken. In here, where the long table-bar had been set up, were almost as many people.

Rex squeezed through the pack and put a sherry in her hand.

"Looks as though there's only a bottle or two left. In half a minute they'll start a stampede. I'll give you a gangway. Cheers."

Thelma smiled, thanking him. Rex was a rat, a rake, a roué; she would rely for her life on Rex Willison as she would rely upon thin ice. But he was big, with magnificent shoulders and a cheerful grin. He was the kind of man she wanted near her, today. Someone who could help her. Rex would help, because it would cost him nothing. If she had to, she could call on him for a strong arm beside her.

Victor had caught the two-fifteen, and by now was past Salisbury. Maurice was at home, over the Sussex Downs. Eve was away for the weekend; and there was no one else, except Rex.

She looked at him with a sideways, tilted glance, wondering what mood he was in, wondering whether he'd take her to dinner after the cocktail-party that was next on her appointments list. She was afraid of being alone, today, tonight, tomorrow; alone at any hour until they found Mervyn . . . if they did.

"On your marks, my lovely."

He pressed away with the empty glasses and came back, easing his camera between elbows and hips, apologizing to a gaunt over-hatted matron whose dyspepsia vanished before his charm.

They went into the main *salon*, he and the woman in green, and took two chairs a few rows back from the long draped T-section dais. They were exactly on time: as the commentator came on to the end of the dais from the curtains and sat at the microphone-table, the sound of voices died. He opened his script and looked round, lifting one hand.

The murmur gave way to a silence almost absolute. Thelma thought: In here I'm safe, among all these people, and with Rex beside me; he'd never come here.

"Lights. . . . "

From the concealed loud speakers the word

fell softly; from the long canopies above the dais, the lights threw down their gentle radiance, tinting the satin of the curtains and the massed heads of the hydrangeas in the gilded tubs.

"Music...."

The trio touched their strings, and a waltz as buoyant as a crinoline came lilting in.

"And on with the show...."

Behind the commentator, the curtains parted.

"Number One ... a tie-silk day-dress in Mediterranean blue, by Jacques Despois...."

The model turned at the end of the dais, her small feet pivoting with neat precision, her smile modest and demure, falling lightly upon the dough-white face of the banker's wife in the front row, and on Mrs. Fitzraven, who was known really to be here to buy, and on the thin girl six rows back with her pen poised over the note-book she had brought here in pride and terror, to her first West End show and for her first magazine.

" ... Note the loose, three-quarter-length sleeves, designed for coolness on all occasions; and the softly draped neckline, eternally feminine...."

The model turned again, allowing the skirt to swirl against her slim nyloned legs.

Thelma thought: If I feel really afraid, later tonight, I'll telephone Victor. Just his voice will comfort me.

" . . . Shoes made beautifully to match, by Norman Lane. . . . "

Rex murmured: "Neat little filly, and pretty footwork. Pity a dress-show's such a contradiction in terms."

" . . . The mischievous little hat is by Michelson. . . . "

The curtains moved, and moved again.

"Number Two . . . for the more junior maid-about-Mayfair . . . a simple style in green seersucker, by Vicki Jensen. . . . "

Or I'll telephone Maurice—Victor's so far away, by now, and Maurice would just tell me to get on a train, and Laura would fix a bed.

Valse Petite —they should have begun with that—perfect prelude for this sort of thing.

" . . . The white cuffs are detachable, and so is the collar . . . and the belt looks just as nice on a different dress, as we shall see in a moment. . . . "

If the worst comes, I can stay near Rex—he'll dine me if I ask him, and I could stay at a small hotel somewhere—somewhere a long way from the flat, where Mervyn would never find me. I needn't really be afraid.

"Want a shot of that one, afterwards?"

"M'm? No, we had copies this morning."

"You feeling all right?"

"Yes, of course."

"Look a bit miserable."

"I'm all right. Victor's gone away on business for a week."

"Wonder if I'll ever meet a girl who'll be miserable when I leave her for a week—"

"You wouldn't be interested in one like that."

"That's true."

The lights dreamed down. The violins played on. The satin and the silk walked in smooth parade along the dais. The banker's wife stared gloomily, and Mrs. Fitzraven made a careful note, and the fashion writer with the dark hair and hazel eyes argued with the fear that was in her mind, that hung like a soft-winged bat in her mind, shut in and shut away from the lights, and the music, and the swing of silk.

Her heels sounded with a faint echo along the pavements by the wall . . . the heel-tap, bone-tap of a skeleton along a coffin lid.

She stopped, and drove out the sly morbid simile, dismissing it with an effort that was not easily made. Then she walked on, towards the block of flats. Walked on, with the heel-tap, bone-tap—no—my footsteps, only my footsteps, over the paving-stones. He won't be here. He wouldn't dare to come here. All over London, all over England, they're looking for him. Everywhere.

She turned the corner, and now saw the building where she must go in. From this corner to the building the distance was about a hundred yards. Four street-lamps stood at intervals, lofty and remote. Between the second and the third a saloon car was parked, its red eye wakeful below the rear window. Two more cars stood at the curbside, farther on, facing this way. No one was moving in the street.

She walked slowly, the rhythm of her heel-taps slower than the beating of her heart. Rex had gone on to the Studio Club after their dinner; she could have gone with him, and almost had; but she had to return here tonight, at some time tonight, even if only to pick up her night things and leave again, to stay at an hotel. At the Studio she would have been restless, dreading the moment when she must leave. Now she had got it over; and there were only these hundred yards to go.

She had nearly come in a taxi; but in a taxi she would have been hurried to the entrance of the flats, without a chance of watching the street as she watched it now, her eyes searching the doorways and the drivegates, the shadows and the parked saloons.

She knew why he had got out, in the early hours of this morning. His reason would bring him here. Already he had found her new name: Marjorie had told him, on the telephone. He would have looked for Tasman in the directory; and although he could not be sure that one of the few addresses there was hers, he would try to find out, and would hurry; because his freedom might not be long.

She walked on, nearing the bright red eye of a

rear-light. The car was empty as she passed it.

Above the chasm of the street the sky was cloudless, but there was no moon. The air was calm, the small sounds carried clearly to her ears: the tiny creaking of the cooling-system, beneath the bonnet of the car she had just passed, as the hot metal contracted slowly after the tumult of the engine's movement; the slight clink of a chain as a dog stirred outside its kennel in one of the nearer gardens; the high faint pealing of a piano, drifting through the partly open window near the eaves.

A cat moved and her hand flew to her throat and her fright was nearly voiced as the flash of fur sprang down from the gatepost and darted for the shadows. The two animals had met in the starlight, and each had been afraid.

She passed the driveway of the tall Nash house, and came abreast of the railings near the block of flats; her heart still hammered to the aftermath of fright; her footsteps were quicker than before. As she came to the entrance, walking into the pool of light on the paving-stones, she knew suddenly that she had reached a point where she was trapped. If he came for her now, she could run nowhere without hearing him run behind, faster than she.

Standing motionless for a moment in the pool of light, watched by the man in the doorway opposite, she forced herself to name her fear. It was not of the night nor of man: the night was not dark here, but in places brightly lit; and man was of her own kind, capable of harming her only physically, and she was not a physical coward. It was not the fear of the supernatural that was in her, for she had never been frightened as a child by talk of bogey-men or ghouls or ghosts; nor did the thought of death make her afraid, though she respected its danger and avoided its everyday threats. What, then, was left—fear of what?

The fear of the mad, of the mind deranged. Fear of Mervyn.

Even the thought of his name sustained the fear, even now as she reasoned the matter out, here in the lamplit street. And she feared not only that his mind was mad; she knew why he had escaped, and in that certainty was the other consciousness: of death. If he came here, it would be to slaughter her, with the same strange hideous strength that had strangled the woman on the bombed-site, in Ludgate Hill.

As she turned up the steps to the entrance of the block of flats her nape was creeping, as if she were aware of the man who watched, in the shadows across the road.

5th

MOVE

♛ THEY WALKED along Cannon Street, hearing the exhaust note of their taxi die away. Bishop said:

"We're not far from Queen Street. The Tasman flat is in Thames Gardens, round the corner."

They passed a telephone box, and Frisnay said:

"How much of what you've told me is reliable?"

Bishop shrugged.

"How reliable is Miss Gorringe?" he said.

Frisnay stopped, and went back a few paces, opening the door of the telephone box. Bishop waited outside, strolling patiently on the lamplit pavement, lighting his pipe and watching the smoke go drifting in the still night air. When

Frisnay came out, Bishop said:

"Going to watch the flats?"

"Yes."

They walked on, together, their feet quiet over the paving.

"Going to call on Thelma Speight?"

"No."

"Why not?"

"How do we know if she's helping Speight or not?"

"I don't think she is, Freddie. Reason it out. She goes abroad after the trial, and comes back a whole year later with a man who's her new husband, except for the little detail of the ceremony. Why help Speight? She might be sorry for him, but the girl's had enough of a time as it is, seeing her husband convicted at the bar, and knowing what he did to the Martin woman. If she saw Speight, now, I think she'd turn him in."

"We can't rely on that," Frisnay said. "I think you're right, but we can't rely on it. We can keep just as good a watch on her without knocking on her door."

"Has she knocked on yours?"

"What d'you mean?"

"I mean has she asked for police protection, since the news got out that Speight was free?"

"No. Why should she?"

"She might be scared."

Frisnay said: "About what?"

"Picture it: suppose Speight has got to hear about Tasman. I know he's been in Broadmoor and the walls are high; but news gets in and out of places in a lot of ways. Gorry's certain he wrote to his wife, care of Eve Jordan; probably his wife wrote back. She might have been indiscreet—"

"Would Speight expect his wife to wait for his release—which might never come—and live a celibate existence indefinitely?"

"Put yourself in the place of a man committed to an asylum on a capital conviction, Freddie, and even call him sane except for neurotic outbursts—and there's nothing you might not expect of your wife or the world outside. Intense jealousy wouldn't be unthinkable in a man like Speight."

On the corner of Queen Street they stopped. Frisnay looked along the street towards the Thames.

"You think she might be in danger while Speight's loose?" he said.

"Anyone might be. You know that. There's a homicidal maniac at large."

Bishop turned away. "I'm leaving you here. I've had a thought. Good hunting."

He left Frisnay standing at the corner. As he walked slowly back along Cannon Street a black saloon with radio antennae passed him, nosing with a quiet deceptive speed under the standard lamps. It swung into Queen Street and slowed as Frisnay moved towards it.

Bishop walked on. From this moment there would be a police surveillance of Thames Court. If Speight tried to see his wife there, they'd get him. But Bishop had his thought, the idea that had come to him as he and Frisnay had driven up Ludgate Hill in the taxi, minutes ago. It might be boring, but it had to be tried out.

He went into the phone kiosk that Frisnay had used, and dialled his King's Road flat.

"Gorry?"

"Yes."

"Did you send it?"

"Yes. It's there by now."

"D'you mind staying in, in case there's a call?"

"I wouldn't miss it for anything. I'm becoming interested in this case. So are you."

"It's taking some sort of shape. I've just left Freddie; he's moved two men into Thames Gardens on a twenty-four-hour shift-watch. I've also just had an idea, and it might keep me most of the night—"

"Dangerous, Hugo?"

"Yes, there's a slight risk of varicose veins. It means standing all the time. Sweet dreams."

He came out of the telephone box and walked towards St. Paul's. It was nearly ten o'clock and London was in the doldrums, while Act Three reached its grand climax (though the critics wouldn't admit it in the morning) in the West End theaters, and the projectionists ran the last reel of the feature in the cinemas, and waiters leaned against the wall and watched the clock while the last half-dozen diners sat to their hamburgers and chips.

Along Cannon Street and a couple of hundred other streets the taxis crawled, a vast and scattered school of luminous fish along the channels of the Metropolis, waiting to pounce on the willing minnows of the crowds as they teemed from the theaters, and the cinemas, and the restaurants.

At this moment, London was out. Soon, it would want to be taken home. Meanwhile, there was this lamplit lull, most suitable to Bishop's purposes.

He passed St. Paul's, and then Ave Maria Lane, and then Pilgrim Street; and then vanished.

Her shoe touched something as she turned to close the door; it scuttered with a small dry sound across the carpet, like an indrawn breath. Her own breath blocked in her throat and she swung round, wide-eyed and with her nerves icing.

In the glow of the ceiling lamps she saw the envelope, mute and white against the royal blue of the carpet. In a moment, when her breath was free again and her nerves melting back to life, she closed the door, and listened with a sharp relief to the snap of the Yale.

Then she turned to face the room, and the

white envelope. It stared up at her, oblong and blank but for the three penned words: *Mrs. Victor Tasman.*

She did not move. She saw Mervyn, speaking from a telephone box, listening to Marjorie's quick little sparrow voice: *We know no Speight. Our beauty-editor's Gloria del Ray. In private, Mrs. Tasman. Sorry. Try Criterion Press.*

Mervyn's wide, stubby-fingered hand would have dropped the receiver on to its rest, would have picked up the S-J directory. Tasman Dress Agency ... Dr. B. J. Tasman. M.R.C.S ... Victor Tasman ... Victor Tasman of 53 Thames Gardens, EC4.

Here. This room, in this flat.

She narrowed her eyes, trying to recognize the handwriting on the envelope. It was not familiar. It was not Mervyn's; but he might not have written the envelope. Just the note inside.

For a moment she pressed her shoulder-blades to the door, looking with a slow glance round the room, at the tiger-stripe suite and the limed-oak draughtsman's table that Victor had left in perfect tidiness. The book she had been reading was still on the arm of the chair; the long dress-box was still on the settee as she had left it; the curtains were still as she had moved them this morning.

No one had been here in her absence. Even at this moment, with her nerves alerted for alarm, she sensed no hint of intrusion in the room.

She straightened her tensed body from the door, and moved towards the envelope, picking it up. The Pink Lightning lacquer of her nails flashed under the lamps as her fingers ripped at the envelope. The note was not from Mervyn. It was brief:

If you need help, telephone Bishop at CAR 2330.

She read the words three times. They were composed beautifully, in a generous, feminine hand. She did not understand; but she held the paper tightly, taking it to the settee and sitting there beside the dress-box, conscious that the message meant good, and not evil. She did not know the name Bishop; the telephone number was strange; but someone called Bishop knew her, and her address. She had imagined, until this moment, that only two people were aware of her real name—Speight—and that only they shared the secret. Eve Jordan and Maurice Jerrold. Now there was a third. Bishop. A woman, by the handwriting.

Somewhere in London, someone—a stranger —realized that she might need help.

She screwed the note and envelope into a ball, and dropped it into an ashtray, committing the telephone number to memory. She might dial it, tonight, tomorrow, the next day; but only if she were desperate. At this moment she was merely frightened, more by her overworked imagination than by the threat it fed upon. But the threat was real. She had known, since the last visit she had made to Broadmoor, that Mervyn would try to escape and would try to find her. And if he found her, he would kill, as he had killed before; but this time with a motive, a sane reason driving an insane mind.

She shivered, and switched on the electric convector, though the night was warm; but after she had made coffee, and had curled up on the settee to drink it, she still felt chilled, and uneasy, and afraid. Somewhere in London was Mervyn, too, prowling . . . no, not prowling—walking, merely a man walking; but a madman, in all truth a madman, with murder on his hands . . . and another in his mind.

She got up quickly, testing the Yale catch and going into the bedroom. The door to the iron fire-escape was bolted; the windows were closed and latched. Through them she stared down across the lower roofs to where the river went, dark and silent beneath the bridges, beneath the stars. She saw no one in the area immediately below, or in the narrow gardens, or anywhere outside. Down in the gloom she could not make out the shape of the man who looked upwards at the block of flats.

He saw her turn from the lighted window, and in a moment the light went out. He waited on, patiently, as he had been trained to do at Hendon.

Thelma went back to the sittingroom, turning the lamps out and going to the window. The two cars were still parked at the curbside; two people—a man and a woman—walked down the pavement opposite, arm in arm and talking quickly; even through the window-glass she caught the faint sound of their voices. She watched them go and turn the corner, feeling that she had lost friends that could help her if Mervyn . . . don't think about Mervyn.

She left the window, and a moment later the man in the shadows below saw the lamps go on again. He waited on, patiently. Those were his orders, unless Speight came.

When an hour had passed and she gave in to the mounting tension of her nerves, she picked up the telephone, dialling a Hampstead number. The burr-burr began, and went on while she waited, perched on the arm of a chair and smoking a cigarette, phrasing in her mind the first words she would say; until she knew that the words would never be said, because the burr-burr was going on with its monotonous negative answer. Eve was away.

Thelma put on a housecoat, and took the book from the arm-chair, and took it to bed, smoking three more cigarettes before she laid the book aside with less than two pages read. It was nearly midnight and the street was quiet outside. The dance music from the radio in the flat below had stopped. People were going to bed, leaving her wakeful and alone. Lights were going out; doors were being locked; all over London the traffic would be ebbing away into mews and garages and suburban roads. Soon the city would sleep, save for a few people who worked on because some work must never stop, and a few others who had nowhere to go, and a few who had waited for the coming of the deeper night for reasons of their own: thin men with sallow faces; men with quiet feet; men who looked upwards to deserted balconies, a jemmy in their hands. And other men, odd men, who were abroad for reasons that were not simple, even to themselves. Among them Mervyn . . . don't think of Mervyn.

She lifted the telephone for the second time, dialling for trunks. Bristol came through within four minutes, at fifteen seconds to midnight.

She sat on a foot-stool by the telephone, facing the door and the window, her back to the bookcase along the wall.

"Hello?"

She was almost startled by the masculine voice, here with her in the room.

"Victor, is that you?"

"What's wrong?"

So even her voice, even at this distance along the wires, carried a note of fear.

"Nothing, darling. I'm—sorry it's so late—"

"It's only twelve. But I thought you sounded a little—worried."

The familiar voice, changed only slightly by the long-drawn medium, was questioning.

"No, Victor. I'm all right. I just wanted to say good night. That's all."

"Bless you. I was going to phone, but for the last two hours I've been talking my head off, trying to fix a deal."

"Any luck, darling?"

"Not sure. They're sticky; but they're not the only ones. Don't talk about business. I've missed you since I left."

She kept the earpiece tightly to her head, and tried to let it mean something, that he had missed her already. But across the room she saw the blank cream panel of the door. If Mervyn came, he would stand on the other side, lifting his hand to the—

"Thelma?"

"Have you, darling?" she said quickly on a breath.

"There's still something wrong, in your voice. Are you alone there?"

She looked away from the door, because the door was her fear, and the fear was in her voice. She had to reassure him, or he'd go to bed worried.

"No. Eve's here with me. You know what she's like when you try to have a private conversation with your husband—"

"Tell her to go and fetch herself a glass of water—"

"Imagine Eve drinking water."

"Well, she can't hear me, and I'm alone. I've missed you every minute, sweetheart. Bristol's the hell of a way when there's someone like you in London."

"Don't be away longer than a week, Victor. By the end of a week I'll—"

"Have you finished?" the cool remote voice cut in.

"No, we're still talking—"

"Operator—"

"Your three minutes are up—"

"But this is a private phone—"

"I'm sorry—you booked three minutes. Shall I extend it?"

"Yes—no—"

Victor said: "All right, darling—get a good night's sleep. I'll phone in the morning—"

"Yes, Victor—yes, please—"

"Good night, Thelma—"

Desperately she said: "Victor, I'm—" and held her breath, her words, her fear. "Bless you, darling."

The line went dead.

She held the receiver for a moment, as though she could keep his tender voice with her, keep the loneliness away just by holding the smooth, black, mechanical instrument. Her shoulders were slack, and her feet tucked under her on the stool; her head was tilted down a little as she looked at the receiver, so that the soft dark hair hung forward over her brow, its shadow on the wall. The pale curve of her face and the poise of her head gave her the appearance of a young child, motionless with the possession of something precious that she longed to keep her own.

She moved, and her hazel eyes lost the memory of Victor's voice. She put the receiver gently on to the cradle of the telephone, and took her hand away; and she was really alone again; and midnight was already past.

She looked at the door, and, because it was now past midnight, a morbid fancy flickered along her nerves and showed her the door-handle turning, the black lever moving down with its shadow moving behind it over the bright, hard paint-work.

She closed her eyes, knowing that it wasn't true: the handle had not turned; but when she looked at the door again she knew that at any minute she would really see the movement of the long black lever, and hear the soft fumbling of the stubby fingers at the panels outside. It would happen the instant she looked away from the door. It would happen when she was not ready, or when her back was turned, or when she went into the bedroom and tried to sleep. It would happen as she slept.

She drew a breath into her lungs with a conscious effort, and got up from the stool, her fingers fretting among the smooth white cylinders of the cigarettes in the Japanese box until she managed to select one, and light it, drawing the sweet, raw smoke deep into her fear to blanket it.

It was now that Thelma crossed a borderline dividing reason from obsession, and the change of mental territory—from that of control to that of submission—sent her mind amok among a wilderness of terror. It was now no longer possible for her to believe that Mervyn would not come; or, when he came, that he could not get in; or that a Yale lock was any barrier against a man gone mad.

It was no longer possible for her to believe that in these windows morning light would sometime come; or that in this room there would be discovered anything but a strangled cadaver, once herself; or that she would live tomorrow. This was to be her last night among the living, and she would spend it here alone, and cold, and helpless, until the fingers fumbled like small mad beetles at the panels of the door, and the handle moved, and the door opened, and Mervyn stood there, his eyes bright with unreason and his shabby figure slack, and his hands hanging loosely until he lifted them and came to her, bringing his hot, mad hands to her, because of what her fates had decided long ago: that this woman's life would begin in her mother's womb, and end in these two hands.

This certainty was now lodged into her mind, and in a strange way it brought relief: she had no longer to think desperately what she could do when he came, no longer to doubt that she could defend herself against his killing throat-lust, no longer even to wonder if he would come at all. She had submitted, almost as a suicide submits to the closing of the waters or the fierce plunge to the street. She had no longer to fight, to fear, to protest that she wished to live. She had only to wait.

The clock alone recorded that in this room two hours had passed since her obsession had taken control of her; for she had not moved. When she had finished the cigarette she had sat down on the foot-stool near the telephone, and leaned her shoulder-blades against the bookcase, and watched the door: a fey mind waiting for the coming of its last lover, death.

For these two hours, between midnight and two o'clock, there had been no sound in the room, nor any movement. Sometimes a faint echo had come to flutter against the windows' glass—the distant murmur of a late vehicle along the street or the strange fur-throated voicing of a cat, marauding for a mate. But she had not heard these sounds. Outside the window, they were outside her life, in the world to which she could never get back. Sometimes a fan of light had spread across the ceiling, thrown upwards from a taxi's lamps as it had turned the corner. She did not see the path of it across the quiet plaster, it came from the other world.

For these two hours, while the city slept, she had sat on the stool, her slim body sagging against the spines of the books, her face white and without expression, her eyes staring at the door where death would be coming in.

Into this silence came now, at last, a sound. As if its sudden vibration had set off another in sympathy, like an electric shock along a human nervous circuit, Thelma screamed, and drowned even the shrill of the telephone by her side.

6th

MOVE

THE FLOWER grew against the sky, black and many-petalled, with a stem as thick as a tornado's rope, but motionless. Between two of the petals, each as great as a cloud, there gleamed a star.

So close to his eye grew the flower that he could distinguish, along the great black silhouetted stem, the frieze of downy vegetable hairs that sprouted from the stem's flesh; and starlight sheened these hairs, and silvered them. The plant covered half the sky, viewed as he viewed it from his cramped position against the wall; but it was the area of ground in front of him that he watched, and not the sky. It was an area of desolation, enclosed within buildings and windows and spired and spires and tall lamp-standards, an area much like an oasis within the dusty city's desert, for here there grew more plants among the broken brick-work and the bruised foundation-stones than among the buildings that had escaped the bomb, nine years ago.

Hunched against the wall, his legs thrust below an outcrop of masonry, his back pressed to the cool stone, he surveyed the area with a gaze that was now tiring a little, with eyes that thirsted for movement to break the monotony of this unchanging scene. Sometimes he looked upwards, and watched the great plant that the nearness of his eyes transformed from a simple wisp of London Pride to a giant beanstalk taller than the Milky Way; and then, his eyes refreshed by movement of their own, he watched the ground again.

Midnight rang down from the nearest spire, and he counted the strokes, and for amusement tried to mark the instant when the sound of the last dying chime was really gone; but he failed: the final vibrations ebbed away with such a liquid dissolve of sound into silence that it was impossible to tell when the change was made.

He gave in at least to the rigors of this monotony, and filled and lighted his meerschaum pipe, shielding the flame of the match with his half-prone body. After the long vigil, this little action came as eventually as a sudden attack launched against a garrison in the silence of a never-ending night. He sat back, puffing at his pipe, dispelling the first rich smoke with his hand, until the burning tobacco settled to a glow.

Twice already, since coming here, he had almost got to his feet and gone away, because the chance of success was worse than poor. But he had resisted the temptation to give up by repeating in his mind the thought that had brought him here, to the bombed-site in Ludgate Hill: *often a murderer revisits the scene of his crime.*

Somewhere here, among the rubble and the creeping tapestry of weeds, Joanna Martin had been found, with the life throttled from her body and her blood congealing on the slab of stone that her skull had split against, like a snail-shell hammered by a bird. And they had found Speight, too, lying in the half-choked cellar, below the woman's body, still unconscious from his crashing fall after the frenzy of the kill.

Either mute stones are infused with memory, like an unseen stain, or Hugo Bishop allowed himself the mental action of picturing the scene to divert the boredom of his vigil; for he found his thoughts wandering, not away from this place, but back in time, to the night of two years ago when Joanna Martin had been slain.

He saw in his mind, as he crouched here, the movement of her dress as she fled across the weed-strewn masonry, turning white-faced to see the man who picked his way among the bomb rubble; saw the shadowy figure of Speight as he reached the girl and touched the prey he would kill; saw the gleam of her eyes, terrified in the starlight, and the fling of her hair as her body was thrown down against the jagged stones; saw Speight, driven onwards by blood-lust, lurching with his thick, square hands to do the thing that, but for a trick of chance, he would have loathed to do had his brain been whole.

In Bishop's mind the kill was made again, a swift dark rush of movement and a shock of agony, the fierce lock of fingers upon flesh and then the beat of bone against the stone and then the blood, creeping in tendrils of dark, sickening crimson over the granite pillow that the bomb had fashioned for her head. And she was dead.

Poor Speight...born, reared and fated for this hideous climax, without a chance of choosing to be stillborn, or born at least not destined to be mad.

Bishop raised his eyes again, and squinted through the flower to the stars. The vigil had made him morbid; the stones against his back had made him cold; and for the third time he thought of leaving here, and leaving the memories of the place to brood alone.

As he moved to ease the cramp in his leg

the range of his vision was enlarged, and he turned his head to look almost directly above him, where the stars roofed a gap in the broken walls. For a little while he did not speak, or move again; and then, as the first flush of the shock receded along his nerves, he said softly:

"Hello, Speight."

The silhouette remained immobile, and only the angle of its head told Bishop that the eyes in the shadowed face were watching him. How long they had watched him, and how long Speight had stood over him here in the deeper shadows, he did not know. His reverie had lasted perhaps for ten seconds, and it must have been while his mind was ranging over the murder scene that his vigilance had relaxed. One thought made him furious with himself. He should never have lit his pipe.

He remembered Gorry's question, on the telephone: "Dangerous, Hugo?" Yes, it was dangerous, here now, suddenly. He had crouched against this wall for two hours now, and his legs and spine were cramped. His position alone had him at a disadvantage, for Speight was standing almost directly over him, after coming up from behind, across a flat area of stone.

This man had done murder here already; and now that he was free, all men were his enemies; and even a mad mind would know the logic of it.

Bishop's quiet voice came again among the

brooding masonry, the starlit weeds.

"What's it feel like, being out?"

The big man did not move, though Bishop was as ready as his cramped limbs would let him be. Speight could lift a foot and crash the shoe down against his enemy's face; or he could swing a foot back and smash a kick towards the head; or he could simply drop, flinging himself across Bishop with the squat hands groping for the windpipe, as once they had learned to do. But he could do nothing without a preliminary: the lifting of the foot, or the swinging back of the leg, or the body-drop. Any of these preludes to attack would give Bishop a fifth-second to defend himself. It wasn't long, but it might be the saving of his life.

From the big silhouette, down from the shadowed face with its frame of stars, the words fell to Bishop's ears:

"Who are you?"

Bishop felt a slight relaxing of his tension, and he ceased to be an animal with wits and nerves and sinews keyed to the theme of instant danger to its life; because Speight's question was reasonable, and there had been sane reason in its tone.

"You don't know my name," he said.

"Tell me."

"Bishop."

"A police-detective."

"No."

For a while Speight said nothing, but kept his head motionless, his eyes never for a moment leaving the man who crouched below him. The silence crept across the rubble after Bishop's last reply, and a zephyr moved, touching the sprig of London Pride in front of Bishop's eyes, so that as the petals moved they blotted out a hundred cosmic systems in the instant, then exposed them again to the man who lay on the earth.

"I can't see much of you," Speight said, "but you're not a tramp."

"No, not a tramp either. I'm a waiter. I've been here a long time, waiting for you."

Above him the big head shifted angle, but though Bishop still failed to glimpse the eyes in the silhouette, he knew they were watching him still.

"Waiting for me?"

"That's right."

"How did you know I'd come here?"

"I didn't."

"You thought I might?"

"Yes."

"Why?"

"To look the place over. This waste of bricks has been the most important place in your whole life. The most important thing that ever happened to you happened here. It's natural for you to come and look at it again, now that you're free."

Speight said with a sudden fierce impulse in

his voice: "I don't need humoring."

"You asked me why I thought you'd come here. That is why."

Ignoring him, Speight went on: "I'm not mad. I was never mad. Don't humor me, that's all. I can't stand it." Silence came in again for a little time, then: "I'm not mad." He said it with the intensity that a condemned man might have used to the padre entering the cell: "I'm not going to die, you can't hang me."

Bishop said: "Can I light my pipe? It's gone out."

Again Speight said nothing for a moment, and for a moment Bishop thought his question had not been heard; then the big man sat down suddenly, his silhouette crumpling like a toy balloon-man with the wind escaping. A yard from Bishop, and facing him, he said:

"You're a policeman, so you won't be armed. Light your pipe."

"If I were a policeman, I wouldn't be smoking."

"I don't care much who you are. You're a damned fool to smoke when you're trying to catch someone in a place like this."

Bishop pulled out his matchbox, nodding.

"I think we've solved my identity at last. I'm a fool." He struck a match. "It could have cost me my life."

In the flame's flare he squinted at the big man, recognizing the square face with its low hair-line and deep-set brown eyes, the irregular bone construction of the nose, and the narrow humorless mouth. Bishop had looked at these features a few hours ago, when Miss Gorringe had shown him the photographs.

"How d'you know you're out of danger?" Speight said. His eyes were narrowed against the bright match flame, raking Bishop's face and trying to recognize it.

Bishop drew on the tobacco, and doused the match. For a moment the gloom was intensified, after the glare of the flame.

"If you wanted to kill me you'd have got it over by now. And while I don't like to under-estimate my capacities, I think you'd have had an easy job, finding me off my guard and on the ground."

Speight said: "Why should I want to kill you?"

"To stop my turning you in, and getting you sent back. Another killing doesn't mean a thing to you, as far as the consequences go. They can't do anything worse to you than they did before. You'd just go back."

After a while Speight said:

"You've worked it all out."

"I've been sitting here for two hours, thinking about you."

Speight began scratching his left hand slowly in the returning flush of starlight, looking down at his hand and scratching it with slow, harsh movements of his fingers. When he stopped he said wryly:

"The place where I'm putting up is a bit of a hell-hole. Riddled with bugs. You can't get out of Broadmoor and stay at the Ritz, even if you've the cash."

Bishop said:

"I can put you up, if you like. There aren't any bugs."

Speight watched him in the gloom.

"I can stand being bitten because my place is a safe place, and if I'm careful I shan't be caught."

"You'll be caught sometime, Speight."

"Not if I'm careful. When I've done what I got out to do, I shall give myself up. I shan't have to be on the run for the rest of my life."

Bishop smoked in silence. A question now would wreck the chance of hearing more. Speight hadn't been able to talk to many people since he had taken his freedom. He was in the mood to talk now.

"You can't imagine what it feels like," he said, "being outside." His voice was quiet, and he spoke slowly, thoughtfully. "Inside Broadmoor it isn't bad. After a year and a half I was transferred to the Club. Have you seen inside?"

"No."

"The Club's a block for privileged advanced patients. We have parole-cards, and we can shave. The others can't shave, but they can use barber's clippers if they want to. Most of them do. Most of them try to look their best, but you can't do much with clippers; it leaves a stubble, of course. But I can shave, with a razor and soap."

Bishop was watching the dark, square face, watching the faint gleam of the eyes: he heard the strange note of pride in the brooding voice. Speight was all right, because he could shave, with a razor and soap and everything.

Something touched Bishop's heart, but he quelled the emotion, because pity for a man like Speight was dangerous, here. He sat with a homicidal maniac, after midnight in a deserted place.

"The Medical Superintendent's a good chap, too. He's president of our chess club and I mated him three days ago, in six moves. He nearly resigned."

If there were a faint smile on Speight's mouth, Bishop could not distinguish it in the gloom; but in the next instant he heard the smile vanish, if it had ever been there.

"It's not bad inside, except that it's a man-trap." He spoke more quickly now and an excitement came burning into his voice as he began heaping word on word, kindling the rage that had started in him. "It's a trap with men in, men and women, all living and eating and sleeping and doing a lot of things that people outside can do—but it's a trap and it's got bars and walls and doors and locks, and you can never see farther than the trees—you can never realize that there's anything more outside than just the trees, even when you know and remember and think about all there is there outside, all the things you saw before you got into the trap, all the people you knew and talked to and once . . . loved . . . and all the buildings—like these buildings—and the life that went on and took you along with it, day after day when you were free, going where you wanted in the world along roads and fields and oceans and hills and—"

His voice snatched on a breath and the spate of bitterness stopped, except for a last dry echo of his thoughts: "Inside the trap, you can't see the world for the trees. . . . "

Bishop did not speak. As the words had run on, flowing in a torrent from the man's mind and drowning all other things till the flood was exhausted, Bishop could have mastered him, could have swung a blow at the dark, square face and rocked back the poor mad head with a force that would have given him immediate initiative and the chance of following up.

Given the will, he could have taken Speight during the last half-minute. But he had wanted to listen to the rushing of the soft furious voice, and try to see a little more into the deep, dark mind of the man beside him; because only when a personality was under stress, and stripped of inhibition and control, could the real person be glimpsed, even if only for a moment. Speight was more interesting than the most renowned potentate or national hero that had ever lived, because in his stricture he was trying to free himself, not from Broadmoor but from the shell of his civilized identity; and to Bishop the effort was fascinating, not only in itself but in the idea beyond: it might be possible, if he could know the man, the core of the man and the depths of him, to help him, and give him back the world he had lost two years ago, among these bitter weeds.

Softly he said:

"This thing you want to do—the thing you say you escaped to do—what is it?"

Speight's head moved.

"I'll do it alone."

"I'd like a chance of helping."

"Why should you help?"

"I'm only human."

"Then you'll break down. Humans are weak. You wouldn't be able to resist sending me back."

"But you say that when you've done this thing you'll give yourself up, and be sent back anyway. So I could help, without being a danger to you."

Speight said:

"I don't trust you. I don't trust anyone. That's why I had to get out."

Bishop waited, hoping the quiet, bitter voice would go on, and say more; but it was silent. He said:

"Do you trust yourself?"

Speight's head turned.

"I'm not my own enemy. That's all I know. It's all I need to know. Everyone else is my enemy, and I know that, too." Suddenly he was going on, as Bishop hoped he would, without the tenor of his tone changing or the bitterness leaving its quiet cadences: "I suppose you were in London when it happened. Two years ago, when it happened. Maybe you were at my trial, too, when they—"

"No, I wasn't there—"

"I don't care if you were there or not." A quick anger came into the voice. "You're against me —you're one of the enemies, and my enemies were at the trial, so you were there too. You're from the *outside*."

The silence came again, the silence of small sounds: the breathing of the two men; the dry whisper of leaf against leaf as a weed swayed to an errant wing of the zephyr; and the million tiny sounds that a great city makes when it sleeps—a faint voice, far away; a wheel turning; a window closing; a high clock, measuring the night.

When Speight spoke again, his voice had changed, and Bishop recognized a weakening in the resolve of the man to be alone and to trust no one.

"But I wish . . . you weren't one of *them*. I wish there was one—just one. You. I only wish it—I know it isn't possible. Don't think you're persuading me, whatever your name is—what did you say your name is?"

"Bishop."

"You don't look like a bishop, you're too thin and too young—"

"Suppose I were not what you call one of *them*

71

—one of the outside people—"

The voice grated.

"But you are."

Speight's hand moved and Bishop tensed, holding his right arm back and ready for a desperate swing at the dark, square face; because at any moment this reasonable, reasonably bitter voice might shout hate at him, and the quiet brooding shape might become galvanized with the animal desire to kill an enemy, whatever reason said.

"You *are* one of them," Speight said. "But I can show you this, without trusting you."

He held out a square of paper, and Bishop took it. All that he could see in the gloom was that it was a portrait of a head. He struck a match, and in the bright flare studied the sketch.

It was the face of a man, on which Speight had captured an expression with his pencil: an expression that was not easy to look at without a qualm of uneasiness, even for Bishop. In the expression was hate, and fear, and panic. The fine-drawn lines of the eyes and mouth compiled a total of strain that transformed the face of a man to a face of abstract evil: yet there was still character in the portrait sufficient for recognition. If Bishop saw this man, he would recognize him, even though he would not see the hate, or the fear, or the panic. With a pencil on paper, only an artist could fashion this result.

Speight said softly:

"You live in London?"

"M'm?" Bishop gave him the portrait. "Yes."

"I think this man lives in London. Have you ever seen him?"

Bishop said nothing for minutes. The match had long burned out, and Speight had the sketch again; but against the increased gloom Bishop still saw the face clearly, etched in his memory, as he had seen it in the little flame-light a moment ago. He had never seen the face before tonight.

"No," he said quietly. "I've never seen him."

Speight fumbled with the paper, folding it again and putting it safely away. He said:

"I have. I've seen him. And at the time I saw him, he was like that."

"D'you know his name?"

"No."

"When did you see him?"

Speight shook his head. "I showed you the sketch, in case you could help. But I can't trust you to keep anything I say to yourself." He put his arms on his knees, and sat for a moment with his head down, staring at the rubble under his feet.

With one blow, Bishop could take him now. He did not move. He said:

"Speight, you're off your guard."

Slowly the big head turned, and the glint of starlight delineated his eyes as he looked at Bishop.

"That doesn't matter."

"I could have knocked you out a moment ago."

"Why should you?"

"To drag you along and have you sent back."

"But you're not a policeman. I know now, because we've talked. I've talked to too many of them to mistake you for one."

"But I'm one of those on the outside. I'm an enemy."

"Yes, but you're too interested in me—for a reason I don't understand—to knock me out and send me back." He gave a brief, cynical little grunt. "Yet."

Bishop did not move as Speight rose to his feet and stood looking down at him. Speight said:

"Just because you didn't hit me, you mustn't think I'm going to trust you, Bishop." In the slow voice there was a timbre that again touched Bishop's heart, great though the man stood above him, and dangerous as he was. "I can't trust all the people who never hit me. People can hit, without hands. Sometimes without meaning to."

He stood motionless, seeming to think deeply; then his voice went on as softly: "Bishop, I'm going now. If you try to stop me I shall kill you, and throw you where they found the woman."

He moved, half-turning but keeping his head at an angle from which he would still see Bishop, if Bishop sprang. When he reached the jutting remnant of a wall, he stood for a moment with his hands pressed flat to the weathered brick, his head turned fully towards where Bishop crouched.

He heard the low voice, questioning from the wall where the weed grew huge against the sky.

"Speight—tell me what you escaped to do."

The words, soft though they came, echoed for an instant among the scattered masonry. The answer came back as quietly.

"You think I'm mad?"

The shape of him moved again, and rounded the jutting wall, and vanished. A moment later, Bishop heard a stone grate against another; then silence, save for the million tiny sounds of the sleeping city, became complete.

He looked at the huge black flower that grew half across the sky, framed by the web of stars. If he followed Speight, he might succeed in taking him by force; he might not. But he would not even try.

For three good reasons Speight must go, and Bishop, knowing it, relaxed.

The flower grew against the sky, black and many-petalled, with a stem as thick as a tornado's rope, but motionless. Between two of the petals, each as great as a cloud, there gleamed a star.

7th

MOVE

♛ IN THE room her scream had died, but the bell was ringing on with an adamant stridency that pierced her fingers as they flew to her ears and tried to silence it. They failed.

In the sound of the telephone bell there was nothing fearful; but each repeated vibration sent the repeated shock along her nerves like an intermittent electric current. She knew without doubting that it was Mervyn, standing in a telephone box, his squat hand fixed round the receiver. Her fear, which reached its climax now, clung to the obsession it had fed upon, so that nothing, at this moment, would have assured her that it was not Mervyn who was waiting for her to lift the receiver, nothing would have made her believe that if she lifted it she would hear a voice that was not his.

Her fear alone told her that it was Mervyn; but reason would have suggested it too. It was in fact the truth; a mile away and deep among the web of the sleeping streets, Speight was standing in a telephone box, the receiver to his ear, his eyes watching his own eyes in the metal-framed mirror over the instrument.

He thought, as he looked into his eyes, of the man on the bombed-site, Bishop. He thought also of his wife, whose telephone bell was ringing now, if she were there. But there was no expression on his face, as there had been on the face he had sketched two years ago.

In the room a mile away the bell rang on, driving its bright sound-blades deep into the vitals of her terror. When the bell stopped, her terror remained; and she sat for minutes, nursing it, hunched on the stool with her hands still pressed to her ears, still hearing the note of the fiendish bell as if that first shrill shock of sound had been trapped inside her head by her flying fingers, and could not get out.

Then the tension went from her, because she was still conscious, and became—despite her fear—aware that the bell had stopped. As she dropped her hands they felt like the hands of someone dead: chilled, and senseless, and inert.

She raised her head, opening her eyes, and felt sweat crawling on her skin as it dried. Her stomach was numb, sickened by the onrush of the terror. Her left hand moved and lifted the telephone receiver. Her right hand dialled at the instrument with a slow, shivering desperation.

She heard the sound of the bell ringing at the other end of the line, somewhere across London.

Vera Gorringe moved her Queen to Kt-4, and as the shadow of her hand flew back across the chequerboard, the silence was broken by the bell.

On the big desk that spanned half the window bay, Princess Chu Yi-Hsin moved her gentle head, and her sapphire eyes gazed at the telephone. Although the bell that was ringing was fixed to the wainscoting of the wall, the Siamese did not turn her head in that direction; for she knew from experience that when this noise began, either the man or the woman would come to the desk, and talk to the tiny invisible creature that was always trapped in the little odd-shaped box.

Bishop left his chair by the chess table, and picked up the receiver.

"Yes?"

For perhaps two seconds he heard no answer; but he thought he detected the sound of tremulous breathing. Then:

"Are you—called Bishop?"

Miss Gorringe heard the half-muted question from where she sat, and stopped considering how Hugo would counter her Queen to Kt-4. The voice on the telephone could be Thelma Tasman's; if so, the game would be postponed.

"Yes, I'm called Bishop. Are you all right?"

He watched the cat trying and failing to picture the scene at the other end of the wires, preparing himself for any action that might be needed, perhaps urgently. But it shouldn't be necessary. Freddie had his men on the job; and Speight couldn't have got through.

Her voice was steadier, though her breathing was still faster than normal.

"You know who I am?"

"Mrs. Tasman?"

"Yes. I—got your message."

"And you need help?"

The faun-skinned Siamese was watching him, as he talked to the tiny invisible creature trapped in the box; and he stared back, looking into the luminous blue of the eyes and seeing his own reflection there. Many times the cat had tried to stare him out, and sometimes had succeeded; it was a game they played, the human being and the beast each tacitly accepting the simple rules: look away and you lose! But at this moment the human being had too much on his mind, either for chess or stare-you-out. He heard:

"No, I—don't really need help. I just had to ring you."

"To find out who I was."

"Partly."

"And partly for someone to talk to, in the early hours. So as not to feel alone."

"Perhaps. I didn't realize it was the early hours. Were you asleep?"

"No." He looked away from the cat and the cat felt smug: the winner! He said: "What frightened you?"

"Nothing. My imagination, I expect."

"Well, if I were you I'd just turn in and get some sleep. Otherwise you'll—"

"Mr. Bishop, I—wanted to ask you something. A few things. Please."

In her voice he heard a stifled desperation, a fear that he would ring off. He blocked the mouthpiece and sent Miss. Gorringe a glance, speaking softly and quickly.

"Either she's scared stiff or she's got Mervyn Speight with her—or maybe both. Take over and keep on the line for ten minutes."

Into the phone he said: "All right, but give me a few minutes. I've forgotten to put the cat out. I'll hand you over to a friend of mine. Shan't be long."

Vera Gorringe took the receiver from him, and he nodded, going quickly out of the room as she took up the conversation.

"Mrs. Tasman, I'm Vera Gorringe. It was my

writing on the note, and I sent it for Mr. Bishop. Among other strange things, I'm his confidential secretary, so please speak as freely as you wish."

The Princess Chu Yi-Hsin watched the woman talking into the box, and perhaps considered it odd that humans appeared to become excited and active with no visible cause, such as the capture of mice or the discovery of fish. They were a strange species, and interesting to study.

As the voices along the wires maintained the link between King's Road, S.W.3, and Queen Street, E.C.4., a vintage Rolls-Royce began to whisper its way round Sloane Square, heading east and forming a second link between the two districts.

Along Piccadilly the ancient but immaculate machine was sighted by three constables, a lady of Mrs. Warren's profession, and a cracksman on his way to split a peter. Down Fleet Street the side-lamps of the car flashed in reflection across the great ground-floor windows of the Miller-Group building, and the night porter admired the vehicle as it whispered past.

Its driver, the thin young man who was too thin and too young to be a bishop according to an escaped maniac, was not thinking just now of Mervyn Speight. He was thinking that present civilization depended upon delicate mechanism; because Vera Gorringe—whose voice was now passing along the wires a few feet below the wheels of his saloon—was at this moment keeping Thelma Tasman safe from her fear by talking to her, and that depended upon a tiny trembler in the telephone. And Bishop's journey to Queen Street, in his two-ton machine, depended upon the delicate pulsing of the contact-breaker spring in the magneto.

If the trembler of the telephone ceased to work, Miss Gorringe and Thelma Tasman would be separated suddenly by great distance; and if the little spring in the magneto broke, Bishop would be obliged to walk, a primitive man with his feet on the ancient earth.

Yet it was as interesting to consider that the chances of one or the other happening were probably about a thousand to one; and the chances of both happening simultaneously were probably something like a million to one.

The frightened woman of Thames Court was protected by mechanism delicate in the extreme; but it was incredibly reliable.

Bishop reached the end of his odd conclusions, sent the grey Silver Ghost up Ludgate Hill with scarcely a sound from the fabulous engine, and turned into Queen Street.

Mervyn Speight watched the saloon from the shadow of a building in Cannon Street, but did not recognize the driver. Detective-Constable Pratt saw the car draw up outside Thames Court, but did not move from the doorway that concealed him. He'd seen the old Rolls before, when Mr. Bishop had called on Inspector Frisnay.

The murmur of the quiet engine died; the heavy door was opened, was closed. Bishop crossed the pavement and went up the steps. The main swing-doors to the entrance hall were not barred; he passed through and checked the names on the panel, then got into the automatic lift.

His footsteps were audible along the parquet blocks of the third-floor passage, but he walked quietly, reaching the door at the end. When he pressed the bell there was no answer for perhaps a half-minute; then her voice came softly from inside.

"Who is it?"

"Bishop."

When the door opened he found her tensed, and realized she had no proof that in some way Mervyn Speight was not connected with the stranger, Bishop, or that Speight had not—by this means—tricked her into opening her door.

He said:

"Were you still talking to Vera Gorringe when I came?"

She half-turned into the room, slim and still nervous, her small hands dug into the pockets of the blue Dior housecoat, her young, pale face turned to watch him, her head nodding as she said:

"Yes. She told me you were coming, a little

before you rang the bell."

He closed the door behind him and dropped his gloves onto the wall table.

"I felt I ought to arrange an introduction, if only by telephone. In case you were expecting someone else."

The wide hazel eyes flashed over him in a final glance before she turned away, inviting him to sit down. "Will you have a drink?"

"Are you?"

"Not now."

"Then I won't."

She hesitated, halfway between the cabinet and the settee. He offered her a cigarette and lit it for her.

"You mind pipes, Mrs. Tasman?"

She shook her head and managed a faint little smile, sitting down in a chair near him, watching his face as he filled his pipe, trying to think where she had seen him before, or if she ever had. She couldn't remember; yet he seemed to know her, or at least know that she might need help at this moment. He looked carefully at his tobacco and said:

"Is your husband here?"

Her voice had surprise in it.

"No, he's away on business—"

"I mean Mervyn Speight."

Bishop glanced up, catching the expression on her face. It was of slight shock, and a little frightened. She said nothing, but his question had been answered. He said:

"You sounded upset when you telephoned, so I thought I'd just come along and see if everything was all right. I hope you didn't mind. If you do, just tell me and I'll go."

Her right hand was held in her left, with the cigarette between the curled fingers. Half her face was in soft shadow, cast by the wing of the chair. Softly she said: "No, please don't go."

He looked at her fully for the first time, admiring the delicate proportion of her features and detecting the strain at the corners of her eyes and mouth, the tensioned posture of her hands, the unrelaxed attitude of her body in the chair. He lit his pipe and leaned back comfortably on the cushions of the settee, his narrow head turned towards her.

"At this hour, the world's peaceful," he murmured easily. "Let's relax, until you want me to go. On the telephone you said you'd like to ask me a few questions. Please do."

After a moment she said: "It's rather difficult."

"Oh, it'll come, with practice. The first question is, who am I? Well, my name is Bishop, and I live in Chelsea. I've got an old motor car and a young Siamese cat, and, on the whole, I'm pretty harmless except when the laundry's late." His voice went on, softly and easily in the quiet room, and the smoke drifted upwards from his pipe in lazy grey whorls; and she felt her limbs relaxing as she watched him and listened to the meaningless ramble of his words. "And you've already met Vera Gorringe, on the phone. She's a friend of mine and she also keeps me in order and gets me out of trouble and get me into more. Her chess isn't much good, but she does try, and she doesn't mind my cat. That might sound trivial, but it's a great deal. A lot of people hate cats."

The ash dropped from her cigarette; neither noticed it. She did not look away from him, because his attitude, and the drifting pipe-smoke, and the cadences of his voice were hypnotic to her eyes and ears. He added:

"The second thing that bothers you is how I happen to know that you might need help tonight, and why I should imagine I'm the one to give it. That's easy. By chance, I discovered that Mervyn Speight is your husband. It occurred to me that a man who is not himself might want to harm his wife, if he finds out that she is living with someone else. Forgive me if I speak much too personally, but this is a bit of an emergency. So I had a note sent to you, offering what help I can."

He looked solemnly at the nest of ash in his pipe-bowl, and finished quietly: "Since you didn't feel like asking for police protection."

For half a minute silence came, bringing an intimacy to the room, accentuating for each the awareness of the other. Then:

"Are you from the police?"

He smiled.

"It's funny, but I'm always meeting people who think I'm a copper. It must be my feet. No, I'm neither from the police nor of the police. I quite like them, but not sufficiently to make me join up. You must regard me as someone who'd like to do some good."

Quietly she said: "And in return?"

He smiled again, briefly.

"Yes, we're all human. In return I get a chance of seeing life—through other people's minds. I'm fascinated by personal crises when I run out of my own. And the very least I can do is to help where I can. That isn't generous, but at the worst it's honest."

"You take a morbid interest in personal trag-edy, for its own sake."

"Interest, yes. Morbid, no. Academic and con-structive, certainly. I'm glad you feel better now."

"Better?"

"Less frightened and more confident. For two pins you'd throw me out, now I've told you how I tick."

The ash fell again from her cigarette; she stubbed it out, sending him a sideways glance.

"You're a queer person, Mr. Bishop."

" 'All the world's queer, save thee and me; and even thee's a little queer'."

As if she were answering his implied question of minutes ago, she said now:

"I haven't asked the police for protection, be-cause I don't want to go through the kind of notoriety I was given two years ago. When I came back to England I didn't take up my friends again; and with some of them that was a wrench for me; but I wanted a private life again. I have it, almost."

"Except for me and my morbid curiosity."

He looked at her seriously. "Mrs. Speight, I don't think you need help. I thought you might, when Speight got loose. I thought you did, when you got on to the phone tonight. But now I've changed my mind." He uncoiled himself from the settee and stood up. "Excuse me," he said gently.

She got to her feet.

"You're not going?"

He nodded.

"I think I will. Time you had some sleep."

They faced each other, she with the fear of being left alone, and the fear that this man Bishop might strip away the privacy that she had built for herself after coming back from Italy; he with the sudden certainty that Speight was not far away from this room at this moment, and that the woman knew, and was glad. She resented Bishop's intrusion; she didn't want to contact the police. She hadn't left town immediately the news hit the press.

But she had called Bishop to find out what his note meant, how much he knew, what interest he had in the poor murderous oddity that had slipped its cage and was free. The man who could ask for help from his own wife, and get it; if no one interfered.

Bishop found it hard, as he faced her, to mate this reasoning with her expression. She didn't look like a woman ready to hide a lunatic when he managed to reach her; she looked strained, and bewildered, and on her nerves' edge. She said:

"All right, if you feel you must go."

She half-turned taking another cigarette, talking over her shoulder.

"It was nice of you to come, as late as this. I must apologize for telephoning so impulsively."

He struck a match, but she had used her lighter and was facing him again. The shock of the night was over for her. The sound of Mervyn's name still sent a chill to her stomach, for she would always be frightened of the mad; but if Bishop went now, and she was alone, nothing could happen to bring back the first rush of terror that had swept through her twenty minutes ago. It had climaxed, and there was no more panic in her tonight. Even if Mervyn came, she would not feel the terror again so soon.

Bishop took up his gloves from the wall-table, and decided to seize a direct bearing on Thelma Speight's mind. He said:

"When I was talking to Mervyn Speight tonight, he told me he'd escaped—"

"You"—her voice cut in softly and incredulously—"you were talking to him?"

Her eyes searched him; for an instant her breath was held. He nodded.

"Yes. We met. He said he'd escaped because there was something he had to do. He said when he'd done it he would give himself up and go back."

She stood so still and so quiet that the faint tremble of her hands was marked. Bishop said:

"Do you know what it is that he's got to do?"

For a minute she said nothing, but looked away from him to the windows, to the telephone, to the door, seeing none of them; then she turned her face again and looked at him.

"If I asked you to stay and talk, would you?"

"Yes, of course."

She sat down in the chair, her slim body sagging and her eyes closing for a moment. Then she tried a faint smile.

"Sorry. But your telling me that you've met him tonight has—somehow brought him so close to me; and I'm cold."

Bishop dropped his gloves.

"I'll have a brandy with you," he said.

8th

MOVE

WHILE THE two people drank brandy in the Thames Court flat, others were awake, talking and thinking of the same thing, the same man, Speight.

There were the detective-constables, right outside Thames Court. There was a police patrol car in Cannon Street with its driver and wireless-operator sitting in silence, waiting; and there was a second car on the Embankment, where the river cut a sprawling limb from the city, with a mental portrait etched on the driver's mind. Five feet nine inches tall; broad-built; square face and head; brown eyes, good teeth, nose-bridge slightly crooked; dark brown hair. Walks lazily; voice rather deep, educated accent. Last seen wearing cheap brown overcoat, no hat, old brown shoes; but might have changed some or all items. Age thirty-eight; and artist of some professional reputation. Note: he is unusually strong, but not easily provoked *in ordinary circumstances*. Personnel will form their own conclusions and use their discretion in the event of sudden encounter.

A mile from the police saloon on the Embankment, another was gliding along the Strand, with a pick-up call coming through on the radio; but it wasn't Speight.

A newspaper, lying across the gutter down Lamisham Lane and spattered by beer from a smashed bottle, carried the limp sub-headlines still—the ancient news fully seven hours old:

BROADMOOR MAN MAY BE IN LONDON.
The man who escaped from Broadmoor Criminal Lunatic Asylum in the early hours of this morning was still free this evening. He is Mervyn David Speight, 38, an artist.

Road-blocks set up by the Berkshire police and maintained by patrols have been in operation throughout the day; but police believe that Speight has slipped through and made his way to London. Cars and lorries are still being stopped and searched, and bus depots and railway stations are being kept under constant watch.

An Alsation dog picked up a trail near an orchard outside the institution early this morning. It led searchers to a stream, where footprints were found; then the dog lost the scent. Tonight the people of Crowthorne were warned to lock and bolt their doors, secure windows, and keep children indoors after dark. Dogs and walkie-talkie apparatus are being used by the police, and bloodhounds may be brought into use tonight.

This afternoon an officer from Broadmoor went to Luton police station, where a man answering Speight's description had been detained. It proved to be a false alarm.

Extra police have been drafted into salient districts, and special constables called out to assist in the search.

The spilt beer had long ago seeped into the newsprint; the broken glass had lost its wink to a dust-film; the paper and all its news was dead by seven hours. But the search went on; through London and the Home Countries.

Watch was being kept at railway terminals and junctions, at coach depots, lorry depots, garages and car-hire offices. Uniformed and plain-clothed police were alerted along roads and through rough country and woods and commons. Churches, workmen's huts, bus shelters and archways were being watched, searched and guarded. On the Embankment, and in St.

Martin's-in-the-Fields, and in workhouses and institutions, vagrants and unemployed were being questioned and scrutinized; and lorries and vans moving towards Convent Garden and Smithfield were arriving minutes behind schedule.

Since dawn of this Friday, some probably half-million manhours had been spent in the search for Speight. He was still free; and down Fleet Street the presses were spinning in their desperate effort to produce information that could survive for a few swift minutes before it was killed by the telephones in the offices above.

Friday itself was already dead. At half-past two on this new morning of Saturday, long before first light, Bishop said:

"That's all he told me. When he left, he said that if I tried to follow him he'd kill me, just as the woman was killed."

The dottle of ash burned bright in the meerschaum bowl as he drew on it for the last time; then he tapped it out into an ashtray.

"Did you try to follow him?"

"No. There were three good reasons why I shouldn't. Apart from the fact that I was cramped and wouldn't have stood much of a chance."

"What other reasons?"

Bishop stood up and began to wander over the carpet, his hands pocketed, his head titled, his eyes glancing at the girl in the chair.

"Two of them are just intuitive. The third is

more simple. It's about giving a man enough rope."

For a moment she was quiet. Then:

"Or bait?"

Bishop stopped pacing.

"You mean yourself?"

She nodded, cupping the brandy glass in her fingers.

"Yes. This thing he escaped to do—I think it's to find me. And to kill me."

"Why?"

"You thought it out for yourself. Mervyn knows about Victor."

"That's Victor Tasman."

"Yes."

"How did he find out? Did you tell him?"

"In a way. Without meaning to. Will it bore you if I explain?"

Bishop didn't answer.

She went on:

"I forgot for a minute why you came. Now I've remembered. But tell me if you want to make notes."

He gave her a brief smile. She had a right to think he deserved that; and he wouldn't deny it.

"When I went abroad, soon after Mervyn's trial, it was to get away from the ugliness and the cheap rag publicity. And perhaps from the sympathy of friends, which in a queer way was worse. I didn't have a conscience about leaving Mervyn to where he was sent. I didn't have anything—conscience or pity or anxiety or shame. The arrest and the trial had knocked all of it out of me. I felt drained of everything except the need for a new place, where I'd never been, and where I wasn't known."

She finished the brandy, but went on toying with the glass.

"The affair didn't break any love between my husband and me. That had gone"—she shrugged briefly—"a long time before, for various quite ordinary reasons. In Italy I met Victor."

She looked up at Bishop and paused. Then:

"I feel ready to tell you things that I wouldn't say to many people, certainly not a stranger. I don't think I should."

He said: "Well, don't."

For a little while she sat upright in the deep chair, watching him. He wasn't looking at her. At last she said: "I think I will."

He began filling his pipe again, now that the bowl was cool.

"At the time I met Victor," her voice came over-casually, "I hadn't been in love for years. It happened then. I still love him, if anything, more. We wouldn't have come back to England at all, ever, but he had to think of his job. It's good one and he likes it. That's important to a person, isn't it?"

Bishop said: "Yes."

"So we came back to London. I didn't get in touch with any of my friends, or with anyone

I'd ever known. Except for two people, and only two. One of them, whom I'd met during the trial, thought I'd make a good magazine writer. I took up the job and I'm still doing it. I like it a lot, so that Victor and I are lucky. We're happy about everything together, except that he doesn't know. About everything together, except that he doesn't know. About me."

She paused, looking up at him gravely.

"Don't tell him, if ever you meet him."

"You'll have to trust me."

"I do."

"That's unwise. You shouldn't."

"What else can I do? You knew enough about me before now to tell him."

"I didn't know he hadn't already been told—or hadn't found out."

"Victor's a busy engineer. He's happy with me. He hasn't a suspicious nature. I've been very careful."

"Why don't you divorce Speight and marry him?"

She looked down at her empty glass.

"One day, I might. Just now I can't do it. It's odd, but Mervyn needs me"—she glanced up, and her voice was quieter—"needed me more in that place than when he was with me."

"That's not odd at all. But what was his reaction when he heard about Tasman?"

She left the chair, setting down the brandy glass.

"You can judge. He escaped."

"But you can't be certain that that was his reason."

She shrugged.

"I'd been visiting him, about once every two months, since I was back here. And I wrote several letters, and he replied. Then . . . two weeks ago when I was seeing him, I mentioned Victor's name—I'd talked of him several times to Mervyn, but just saying he was a man I knew in my job. This time I made a slip. Mervyn began asking me about him, and I suppose he saw I was on the defensive. That was enough. He didn't say anything more. He just left the room, and I thought he was coming back, but he never did. I left the place without saying good-bye. The Medical Superintendent told me before I went that Mervyn had been morose for days; but whether it was true I don't know. I know I said too much about Victor. And I know Mervyn."

Bishop let the silence go on for a while, then he tested the obvious link.

"Was there a motive for his killing Joanna Martin? A reason that anyone knew about?"

"None that I knew. There was nothing about it during the trial; that was partly why the defense succeeded in getting the verdict it did."

"He hadn't met the Martin girl before?"

"I don't think so. He said he hadn't."

Bishop moved close to her, and waited until she looked up at him.

"You've no reason to imagine he was jealous about Joanna Martin?"

She looked down, but her voice was open.

"No reason, no. But he's jealous about me. I know why he's escaped. I know what the thing is that he has to do."

"Have you had any proof?"

"Proof that he's trying to find me. I'd told him I was working for Miller-Group—I'd told him a lot of things that I wouldn't have dreamed, if the idea of his ever escaping had got into my head. He phoned my office, asking for Mrs. Speight."

"When?"

"This morning. He got my new name from them; they didn't realize who he was. There aren't many Tasmans in the directory. I've looked."

"That he's trying to find you seems normal, to me. He wants to see you, talk to you. It doesn't necessarily mean he wants to kill you."

She swung away, finding an ashtray, turning:

"With my life in question, would you really advise me to ignore Mervyn's escape, and risk his finding me off my guard, some night?"

Bishop looked from the window for a little time, noting automatically the slight irregularity of the doorpost's vertical line on the far side of the street, and recognizing it as a man's sleeve. He knew it was one of Freddie Frisnay's men, but if the girl saw it, she'd think it was Speight. And if the police weren't posted here, she might be justified. Speight knew where she was by now. He wasn't that crazy.

He said:

"No. I wouldn't advise you to ignore it. I agree there might be a chance that Speight has got jealous about you. And that he escaped to let off steam and do something silly."

"What has he to lose?"

He saw her reflection in the window-pane; she stood behind him, her hands clasped again in front of her, with the faint grey vine of the cigarette smoke climbing in growth.

Bishop said: "Nothing. Except a few privileges at the institution."

"He'd exchange them for revenge."

He turned to face her, because, although he didn't mind Freddie reading about this visit in his shadow's report, he just didn't like being watched. By anyone.

Moving towards her, away from the window that was under scrutiny, he said: "Yes. He'd give up a good clean shave for revenge, if that's what made him break out."

His certainty of a few minutes ago had worn thin: his feeling that she was ready to help Speight, perhaps even to hide him, perhaps even here. She still had fear in her, and the invisible, inaudible, intangible climate in this quiet room was saturated still with fear. It was still flowing from the girl as she talked, as she glanced around her. It was an ethereal and insubstantial as the nightmare drowned in the light of the opening eyelid; but Bishop sensed it as surely as a dog senses the fear of an outstretched hand.

He said: "Why don't you go away?"

"Where?"

"Out of London."

"I can't. There's my work."

"But you spoke of a risk to your life."

"People cross roads to their jobs every day. It'd be silly for them to stay at home. It'd be silly of me to go away. Tomorrow I've three new shows to cover."

"The shows must go on—"

"Oh, they'll go on just the same without me there. But Gloria del Ray likes her boss. He doesn't pay her for running out of town, and out of guts."

Bishop smiled.

"Don't look now, Miss del Ray, but your shift-lock's stuck."

She doused her cigarette, reflectively.

"At capital T for Theatrical. I'm still afraid of Mervyn. Mad people turn my stomach upside-down. But just now I'm also a bit ashamed of myself. I gave a rather embarrassing exhibition just before I rang you." She titled her head, looking up from the ashtray and folding her arms. "Let me tell you about that. I was so worked up about things that when the phone bell went, you know what I did? I yelled—"

Bishop said: "I know."

She opened her eyes wider.

"Don't tell me you heard it in Chelsea."

"No. I didn't mean I knew you screamed. But there was an echo of something like that in your voice when you rang me. I even told Vera Gorringe I thought Speight was here."

"I sounded like that?"

He nodded.

She said: "Then I'm more ashamed than ever. Please take it that the timbre in my voice was due to simple flatulence."

"Have you bismuth?"

"I expect so."

"Then fix some and get a few hours' sleep, if you've three shows tomorrow."

He picked up his gloves again, checking his watch. It neared three. He said:

"Will you be all right if I go?"

"Of course. Thanks for coming. I still don't quite know how you add up, but I feel better for talking to you."

He moved to the door.

"I'm glad. If you feel the heebie-jeebies coming on again, you know my number."

His hand, pressing down the lever of the door-catch seemed to operate an electric circuit, for the telephone began ringing, on the other side of the room. Bishop's glance flicked to her face.

She caught her breath; her face muscles had tightened; that was all. He said:

"Shall I take it?"

She released her breath.

"Please."

He crossed to the telephone and picked up the receiver. Very softly, so that his voice should carry as little character as possible, he said:

"Yes?"

All he could hear was that the line was open. There was no voice, no sound of breathing. Five seconds passed. The line closed, and the dialling-tone began.

Bishop cradled the receiver. He said:

"Why not go to bed? You won't get much sleep as it is. Let me relax in here, with a book and my pipe. I'll wake you at nine, before I go."

She stood with her arms still folded, the wide sleeves of the housecoat hanging loosely. He said:

"Would nine be all right?"

She nodded.

"Yes. Yes, thank you."

She turned and went into the bedroom, closing the door. He sat down on the settee, taking his shoes off and swinging his legs up comfortably. As he filled his pipe he heard his mind repeating the five-second silence, then the click, and then the dialing-tone. Something at least could be said to Mervyn Speight's advantage. He wasn't talkative.

9th

MOVE

♛ IT WAS Saturday morning. Half the
working world slept on; or, if it de-
cided to get up, it took a long time shaving, just as
a luxury to commemorate the day. The other half
of the working world caught the train as usual,
because either it was essential and had to do with
gas-mains or banks or buses, or it always worked
on Saturdays or bust, because it was the boss and
business was business, particularly when it was
one's own.

On this Saturday morning, too, the Captain
of the Third Eleven poked his head out of the
dormer window and knew there'd be some fast
ones coming from Wilson, because it hadn't

rained in the night and the pitch'd be like iron.

This morning people raked under the seed-boxes and the lawn-mower cover for the tin of Simoniz, because it was Saturday and the old bus had to look like new. One or two of the old buses would be wrecked before tonight, and some of them would be coffins, because today was the second-worst day of the week for Death on the Road. But at least they'd all be polished.

This morning people woke to a day when they'd be happy (because of the wedding), or depressed (Aunt Clarice was coming), or drunk (because of the wedding again—lots of weddings on Saturdays), or dead (because, statistics said, today was the second-worst day for Death on the Road; and even if you avoided accidents, most murders occurred between nine p.m. and midnight on Saturdays).

So it was pot-luck, like every other morning, only more so. For instance, a man in Balham nearly got knocked down crossing the road, just after nine o'clock. He got up all right, but his wife went and fainted because she'd seen it happen. She wouldn't be nagging him for the rest of the day (everything forgiven, dear), but she'd be at him again come Monday (but why faint, it was plain hypocritical?); but there it was, they'd got their Saturday morning, right in the neck.

In Bristol the firemen got a cat down from a wharf roof after two hours sweating with ladders and saucers of milk; and two thousand men and women began making some more biscuits; and Tasman started off smartly, as he'd rehearsed it the night before.

"Gentlemen, the advantage of the KS-3 twin-stage supercharger is twofold: technically, it's a considerable improvement on the unmodified prototype because the overall coefficient is greater by point seven-five; and, practically, it's a better model simply because it takes ninety minutes to install instead of two hours."

He paused, not expecting a challenge at this early stage, and not getting one. While the pre-amble sank in he took three seconds off and felt a prick of anxiety as his thoughts wandered. Was she all right? Should he go back to town this evening and come back on Monday? If she . . .

"Now to get to details, we have the new method of vaneanchorage. I think you all know about that, but I'd like to explain the actual set-up as regards metallurgy."

Furgiss is looking interested. Not looking bored, anyway, even with that face. If I got to London by midnight I could stay till . . .

"The tensile strength of our new Fleximax aluminum-magnesium alloy permits a shallower vanebed than on the KS-2 model—"

"What's the transverse anchorage?"

So Furgiss is really interested. He'd want fifteen hundred of these. Dear old Furgiss—quick! . . .

"Simply a ninety-degree bridge, Mr Furgiss. We've dispensed with the transverse bolt and saved one-tenth of an ounce per vane, or a total of two ounces per rotor."

That'll shake him. On the phone, her voice had sounded so queer. As if she were . . .

"Centrifugal stress, under load?"

He's really keen.

"Sixty pounds."

Thelma, darling, are you all right?

"Total?"

"Seven hundred and twenty at peak."

I'll catch the three-fifteen. There before seven. Almost for dinner. Almost.

In Reigate, Surrey, they were preparing the jumps this Saturday morning. Meadow Girl had bruised a fetlock on the gatejump two weeks ago, but the Committee said Meadow Girl would just have to clear it today; they weren't going lower, even for the under-ten's.

Sir Humphrey Rotherson was in the High Street, trying to carry the damned shopping-basket with dignity and for democracy's sake; old Jim Fryer was selling the black-and-tan spaniel—best o' the litter—for five pounds (every penny of it profit, but thank the Lord and the bitch's willingness); and Eve Jordan was saying:

"I'm not sure how much I ought to tell you. Mrs. Tasman's my best friend."

Sergeant Bracknell looked patient, sitting in the deck chair and seeming out of place. He wasn't in uniform, but he wasn't dressed for sitting on the lawn under the cedar tree at Mrs. Jordan's week-end retreat. He was dressed for finding Speight. He said:

"Now, Mrs. Jordan, you should know very well how much you ought to tell me. I'm a police officer making an official enquiry. But quite a-part from that, you'll be helping Mrs. Tasman by helping me. We all want to find this man, don't we?"

He looked at her steadily. Mrs. Jordan had a blonde bubble cut and amethyst eyes and a twenty-four-inch waist and a pleasant degree of uplift; and most of this was faithfully recorded by her play-suit. She was intelligent too, but you had to put on a lot of patience with this kind of party. Drive them too rough and they'll zip themselves right up tight and you don't learn a thing. Tacit compliments to pretty people paid a dividend. Sergeant Bracknell was applying this rule.

"So, really, I'm in your hands," he added with boyish candor.

Eve Jordan regarded him gently from beneath her coolie sunhat.

"The case-hardened hand in the chammy glove," she said pleasantly. "But don't worry, I've worked things out while you were talking."

Sergeant Bracknell cleared his throat.

"Not many people know," she said, "that Thelma is Mervyn Speight's wife. I expect you know enough about her to realize why." She offered him an apple. He shook his head. She said: "Mervyn writes to her quite frequently from Broadmoor. He sends the letters to her at my town address. He thinks she lives there. That's all."

She bit her apple and swung one leg idly from the hammock, watching the policeman.

"How long has this arrangement been working, Mrs Jordan?"

"Since Mervyn was sent to the asylum. Victor Tasman's one of the many people who don't know about Thelma and Mervyn." She bit again. "Please bear in mind, during further enquiries."

He nodded.

"I will." He looked away from the swinging leg and fastened his eyes on an innocent rose-bush. "Are you worried about all this?"

"I could be, if I thought about it."

"You don't feel in the mood to think about it."

"Listen, Commissioner, if Thelma needed my help she'd just ask; and she'd have it, and the sky'd be the limit. Before I left town for the week-end I tried to phone her twice, at her flat and her office. I left a message too. And, in any case, she knew I was coming here. It's routine. She knows my number. She'd contact me almost before anyone, if she wanted backing up or looking after. It's no good my pacing up and down the lawn, tugging divots of hair out, until she phones and says she wants some team-work."

"Why," Bracknell murmured, "should she need

help, would you imagine?"

"She mightn't need help, but if I were in her place I'd need cheering up."

"Would she," Bracknell tried again, "have any cause to be afraid of Speight, do you think? While he's free?"

"Well, I don't imagine she'd ask him round."

"You imply she might be afraid of him."

"Let's not imply anything. We'll keep to facts. I know how you boys love 'em. Mervyn was in Broadmoor for murder. He is certified insane. He's now loose. Yes, I'd say Thelma has cause to be afraid of him."

"Yes, we can assume that. It's natural, of course. But do you know of any *particular* reason for Mrs Tasman—as she calls herself—being afraid of her husband? She's visited him at the institution quite often. They exchange letters. That suggests an amicable relationship, taking the circumstances into consideration. Do you think there might be any cause of to feel that his escape offers a *personal, a particular* threat to his wife?"

Eve Jordan stopped swinging her leg and bit the apple to the core, gazing at Sergeant Bracknell's tie. It was so terrible she felt actively morbid about it.

"As far as I know," she said thickly through the last of the apple, "Mervyn thinks his wife is living alone." She jerked the core over the hedge into the kitchen garden. "Is that what you wanted?"

"Not quite. But it suggests that Mrs Tasman wouldn't be likely to hide Speight, or help him to remain free."

"If she did, I'd boggle."

Bracknell nodded.

"That," he said, "is what I wanted."

Maurice Jerrold reached his office just after eleven o'clock. Half the Miller-Group machine was at a standstill on Saturdays, and the other half normally kept running without its editor-in-chief, relying on title editors, feature editors, sub-editors, secretaries and the boy who over-filled the inkpots.

Jerrold sat down at his desk. He was not one of those who had caught the usual train because they were the boss and business was business. He had not really come here to work: he was worried about Thelma; and the best place to worry from was here at his desk, where there were telephones, directories and a staff—if only a week-end skeleton.

His flecked brown eyes gazed at the dial of the main telephone by habit; because worry had to be dealt with by action, and action was more easily started by twirling that dial than by any other method. This electric contact had been opened so many times, in anticipation, in impatience, in confidence, in anger, in routine and emergency. It had dealt with the crucial and the critical, the banal and the bizarre; it had boosted circulation by five thousand and crippled a rival attack; it had once saved the whole of Miller-Group from financial collapse, and once heard a catch in Jerrold's voice because it was an eight-pound boy and both were doing fine.

Now it was waiting again, the little spring-return dial, for the quiet stab of his finger. They hadn't caught Speight yet. Was Thelma all right?

He hadn't told Laura why he'd decided to come up this morning. Laura knew most things about his life, but where Thelma was concerned he'd just omitted a few facts. Thelma Tasman worked for him, for Miller-Group. She had a nice boy for a husband—an engineering representative. Her marriage was happy, and Laura was fond of her and had met Victor too, and liked him. But Thelma had no past, in Laura's mind; no murder, nor madness, nor any husband but Victor. To Laura, as to the public, Mervyn Speight was the man from Broadmoor, the man who had killed Joanna Martin on the bombed-site at Ludgate Hill. He had nothing to do with Gloria del Ray, beauty editress of *Venus*, nor with Mrs Victor Tasman of Thames Court.

Jerrold looked at his telephone, thinking of Speight and thinking of Thelma, and the news in the noon edition of yesterday.

He first dialed for Thelma.

She didn't answer. He checked his watch. The

du Vancet show began in twenty minutes from now; she was probably on her way. He'd meet her there.

He dialed New Scotland Yard.

They came through. He said:

"This is Maurice Jerrold, editor-in-chief of Miller-Group Publications, Fleet Street. Is there anything on the Speight escape from Broadmoor, please?"

The line was changed. A new voice said:

"There's no statement since two hours ago, when a man detained at Southampton was released after questioning. He was not Speight. Enquiries are going on, and we have a lead in the Bristol area, though nothing's established. False alarms are still being received at a dozen an hour, from Dover to Liverpool. May I have your name again, please?"

Jerrold repeated it, and pressed the contact.

He dialed a number in Knightsbridge.

"Kennedy?"

"Yes."

"Maurice. Is there anything on the inside about Speight, from Broadmoor?"

He could hear a teleprinter ticking in the background, coming through on the wires, and a squeal of static cut in occasionally while he waited. All Kennedy didn't possess was a crystal, in that electrically-rigged attic of his.

Kennedy came back. He said:

"Not much. He was sighted last night, just after midnight, near the Embankment. No release on that. Nothing more."

"He's been seen in a dozen places, all over the country."

"But it was really him, last night, cross my cheques."

"How d'you know for certain?"

"It's my business, remember? Why are you interested in Speight? You don't run that kind of stuff."

"It's still interesting. If anything comes up, let me know, will you?"

"You'll be at your office?"

"On and off. Leave a message, but code it."

"All right, Maurice. Happy week-end, and think of me working."

"You can't have it both ways. 'Bye."

He dialed another sequence, listened for one full minute to the dirge of the *burr-burr,* and put the receiver back, tilting his heavy chair.

Yesterday he had taken a shock when he had seen the noon *Standard*; then, when Thelma had turned down his invitation, he had decided to play things her way; she wasn't going to get upset: why should he? But he hadn't slept well last night. He had dreamed of the trial, of the jury, of the face of Mervyn Speight, the square, immobile face that had looked once towards Thelma when the foreman's voice had intoned the verdict of them all. He had woken this morning to conscious worry, and Speight had become fixed in the foreground of his mind.

Because somehow it looked as if Speight had found out about Thelma and Tasman. Or, if he had not found out, there was a danger that he would, now that he was free. He'd try to see his wife. Of course he would. For whatever reason he had broken out, he'd want to see Thelma. Tasman was away in Bristol, and that made it better, but if Speight got through to Thelma, he'd want to know why she didn't live at Eve Jordan's place after all. That one question would set off the rest of the fuse, and Thelma would risk—

He dropped the chair level and got up, his big brisk hands tugging on his gloves. The little dial hadn't given him anything. Perhaps he would do better to go out and find it for himself. When he came back here there might be a message from Kennedy. Or there might be news from someone else. Or they might have caught Speight. In time.

10th

MOVE

♛ MISS GORRINGE spilt a mushroom with her knife, speared fifty per cent of it with her fork, and looked up, as she munched it, to see the arrival.

The arrival took place immediately outside the window. The window of Dirty Bertie's café was halfway between the floor and the ceiling; and when you sat down here in Dirty Bertie's basement, and looked up, munching your mushroom, you saw the chimneys across the narrow street outside. Or, if a dog were scratching its ear (for instance) on the roadway just outside the window, its silhouette would obliterate fifteen chimneys, the roof, and the top three floors of the flats across the street. In brief, you would be looking upwards at an angle of perhaps forty-five degrees.

The arrival, then, took place in circumstances less normal than those in which a motor car would pull up outside an ordinary, ground-level, conventionally windowed café. You would see merely the conveyance arriving.

What Vera Gorringe saw was the side elevation of a Leviathan radiator, agleam with the original nickel-plating, creeping slowly and with ever-decreasing velocity across the window. This was accompanied by an offside headlamp somewhat larger than an infant's Tottie-Pottie and, of course, vertical instead of horizontal and boasting no handle. This also was of polished nickel-plate. There followed a front wheel, with spokes as trim and taut as a Tiller-girl's stays; a front wing, curved lovingly over it and supporting a six-foot flexible tube fashioned in the form of a serpent, which was the hooter; several yards of mirror-polished bonnet; and finally the offside front door and window.

This last remained in view, as the machine had now stopped. Through the window of Dirty Bertie's basement, and through the window of the immaculate 1920 Rolls-Royce Silver Ghost, Vera Gorringe found herself regarding Hugo Bishop.

"Bertie," she called, "another breakfast, if you please. My conscience had returned to trouble me."

Bertie nodded from behind his counter, but

went towards the steps instead of to his kitchen.

"I keep tellin' 'im, but he don't take a blind bit o' notice, Look 'ow dark 'e makes the place with that great charrer!"

Bertie vanished from Miss Gorringe's sight, but his greeting was audible from the street above.

"Be a good boy, Mr. Bishop, an' take 'er down a few yards, eh? Place gets like night in there, with this 'ere."

As the vintage vehicle moved silently forward on the slope, and halted clear of the window. Bertie watched it with mixed sentiments. It was very good for trade, having a car like that standing right outside your basement three or four times a week; on the other hand, it was no good if people couldn't even see your basement at all, lurking behind all that polish. It was very difficult.

Bishop got out.

"So you've got a liver this morning, Bertram. I'll respect it."

Bertie was going down the steps, his plump, rich voice floating up to his customer.

"I got liver, I got bacon, I got eggs. What about two fried eggs, liver an' bacon, mushrooms an' tomatoes?"

Miss Gorringe glanced up as Bishop reached the tables.

"Good morning, Hugo."

He sat down, watching the rotund form of Bertie ambling amiably into its favorite element, the kitchen.

"Good morning, Gorry. I thought I'd find you down here."

"So you remembered your Gorringe, after all this time. The bacon's exquisite. Bertie is blooming this morning."

A pleasant sizzling noise began in the kitchen behind them; and, moments later, there came the smell of coffee. Vera Gorringe glanced critically at Bishop's crooked tie and untidy hair, She added:

"You appear sleepless and forlorn. How is Mrs. Victor Tasman?"

He adjusted his tie and smoothed back his hair. Her critical glance had not escaped him.

"You have the most unpleasant habit," he said tetchily, "of crude insinuation. Usually in the early mornings."

"I insinuate nothing." She buttered her toast and commandeered the marmalade. "As you've spent most of the night in Mrs. Victor Tasman's flat, I merely thought you'd be in a better position than Victor Tasman to know how she is this morning." She applied the marmalade. "Victor Tasman being in Bristol."

Bishop sighed. His urge to sleep was receding, in inverse ratio to the strengthening smell of bacon and coffee from the kitchen; in half an hour he would feel fresh; but just now he was not in the mood for brittle feminine innuendoes.

Miss Gorringe relented, and her tone became reasonable.

"Tell Aunty. What happened?"

"Nothing much. We think Speight telephoned."

"We think?"

"The thing rang, and I answered it. There was a brief silence while the cove at the other end tried to decide who the hell I was, then he hung up."

His grill arrived, and coffee in a big bright brown jug.

"Beautiful Bertie," he said.

Vera Gorringe said: "Nothing else happened at all?"

"No. We talked, of course. Seems Speight's really been trying to find his wife. He telephoned Miller-Group and—"

"How did he know she worked at Miller-Group?"

"She'd told him, one of the times when she saw him at the asylum."

"You think he's found her private phone number too? Obviously she didn't tell him she was living at Thames Court."

"They gave him her new name, at her office. He probably checked the directory."

Miss. Gorringe poured some coffee for him, the light flashing across her finger ring. Her large and rather colorless eyes regarded the stream of amber coffee. She said:

"If it was Speight who rang in the night, why d'you think he did?"

"I should think it was obvious."

"I always overlook the obvious. I realize he's trying to contact her, and can't reach her in person because of Freddie's hounds. But why call her so late?"

"If you really think there has to be a specific reason, apart from his mere wish to talk to his wife, I'd say he wanted to ask about me."

Miss Gorringe nodded and said: "Ah."

"Makes sense?"

"Yes. He was puzzled, meeting you on the bombed-site. It occurred to him afterwards that Thelma might have put you on to his trail. He wanted to ask her if that was right. And who the hell you were."

"Atta-Gorry. We're beginning to feel conscious. Talk some more."

"All right. Did you tell Thelma you'd met Speight?"

"Yes. I had to. She was playing oysters."

"Did you tell her about the sketch he showed you?"

He shook his head, skinning a tomato briskly. He was beginning to feel clear-headed after a night of what amounted to frustrating inaction.

"No, I didn't tell her about that. She might know the face in the sketch; but it's not easy to ask someone to recognize a portrait by a verbal description. It could be the face of one of the jurors, or a witness, or a police clerk, or any-one—even a male nurse at the asylum. It could be the figment of Speight's morbid imagination."

Vera Gorringe said: "You think the sketch is important?"

"I think it might be extremely important. But if it is, where does it fit in? It must fit into the pattern of his trial or his life at the asylum. If it doesn't, I don't think it means a thing. Have we a file on the court proceedings?"

"We have."

"We'll go through it today, then, after I've followed up a lead."

"What lead?"

"I'm going to mooch round Delford Lane, Spitalfields." Miss Gorringe nodded.

"That's intelligent enough to be one of my ideas. I'm sorry you thought of it first."

"Sit at the feet of the great, and one is imbued with the aura of their divinity. But there's something puzzling you."

"There is. What are we looking for, Hugo?"

He sat back, stirring his coffee. The morning had suddenly become clear, as if the sun had come out to dispense mist. He said:

"Not Speight. The police can do that."

"What, then?"

"A reason or a person."

She was with him now. As sometimes happened, these two people found themselves thinking in the same key, and each tone-perfect. She said quickly:

"The reason for Speight's escaping."

"For that."

"Or the person he escaped to find."

"But not his wife. Not only his wife."

"Nor Tasman?"

"Only if it's Tasman's portrait he showed me last night."

She said: "And it isn't. You described it to me. I've seen Victor Tasman. Unless Speight is a bad artist, or is violently out of focus in his memory, the sketch isn't of Tasman."

"Then it's someone else," Bishop said, and drank some coffee.

"So we're looking for a reason *and* a person. They're really both the same."

"That's right. And we've a picture of them."

"Or Speight has. We've just seen it."

"Or I have," Bishop said.

Vera Gorringe poured herself a last cup of coffee and sugared it and said slowly:

"It's odd, Hugo. We started by being concerned about an escaped maniac and his wife. Now we're much more concerned about an unknown person whom we don't know is even alive."

Bishop smiled faintly.

"That appeals to me. God forbid we should concern ourselves with the obvious. I just hope we're not chasing a fairy."

Miss Gorringe drained her coffee.

"If we are," she said, "we'll catch it, and start a theological revolution."

11th

MOVE

DELFORD LANE, Spitalfields, was composed in the main of yells and smells. The yells came from the score of small boys and small girls and small children too dirty and too excited to claim even sex distinction, and the smells came from the small boys and small girls and particularly the small sexless children, from their pets, from their mothers' kitchens, their fathers' pipes, and their communal food center, which was the fish-and-chip shop halfway down the lane.

On this Saturday morning, at somewhere about ten o'clock, a thin man with nondescript light-colored hair and an old tweed suit was walking down the pavement, picking his way among the various groups, teams and associations—the marble-players, the hopscotch-session and the Yellow Talon gang.

"Out the road, mister!"

Bishop side-stepped smartly and avoided being hopscotched into, though the issue was close.

A small girl, her cheeks stuffed with sweets and coy grimaces, pranced alongside for a few yards, looking up at him with bold blue eyes and a winning sucking noise.

"Allo," she managed stickily.

"Allo," said Bishop.

"Where you goin?"

He quickened his pace. Small boys he could get on with. He understood marbles and wounded knees. He had never understood the advances of small and precocious six-year-old females.

"Along here," he said. She was unsatisfied.

"Don't go nowhere," she said triumphantly. "It's a culdy sack!"

"Then I'll stop when I get to the end."

She skipped twice, and the head of the doll she was clutching fell off. She snatched it up, and hurried to regain her lost position beside him.

"You must be soppy," she said.

Bishop walked very quickly now, looking round and hoping to see a small boy who didn't like the little girl. Perhaps there might be one who would feel in the mood to kick her shins, or something nice like that.

"I ain't seen you 'ere before," she said, with a clever suck at the sweets to stabilize their mass.

"You won't see me here again, either," said Bishop. He hurried on.

"Sa-die!" came a shrill interpolation from a basement area. The little girl swung round.

"Aow wot?"

"Yer mum says come 'ere!"

She skipped again, full circle, righted herself, and darted away with a scutter of disorderly feet.

"God bless your mum," Bishop murmured, and slowed his desperate pace. A ten-year-old tough was looking at him now, surrounded by the rest of the Yellow Talon gang.

"Who you lookin' for mister?"

"Never you mind," said Bishop from the corner of his mouth. There was no reply to this; but he thought it a fair example of the unerring intuition of the young: he might have come along this street for a dozen purposes, but the boy had it—he was looking for someone. So little doubt was in the boy's mind that his question had gone one stage further: who was being looked for?

Bishop passed three more of the narrow, mean-faced houses and reached Number 24, turning down the area steps without more than a glance at the number on the front door.

On the lower door of Number 24a there was a knocker, and nothing more. It hung aslant, for one of the anchoring pegs had broken, and a rusty length of iron wire withheld the knocker from complete detachment.

He knocked with it.

On the outer sill of the window there grew marigolds, their flaring blooms already flat and dulled by falling grime. On the dry earth of the box were cigarette ends, match ends and the wheel of a toy motor-car, red as the marigolds with rust.

The window was heavily curtained by grime and by lace yellow with age. The lace would never be drawn; the grime would never be cleared; the window would never be opened. Soon the marigolds would die off, parched for water. Bishop would have liked to fetch a can, and shower the blooms and their foliage so that the petals came up burning orange and the foliage emerald-green, just so that people would see that at least something that was alive at this house was recognized and cared about.

"Yaice?"

He started, turning his glance from the dusty flowers to the face in the opened doorway.

"Mrs. Martin?"

The woman's face, already hard, became suspicious. Fifty years of life in places such as this had taught her caution: caution of strangers, of pleasant speech and pleasant manner, of everything that was not simple, rough, ugly and direct; for her, life was all these things, and she knew their quality for what it was.

She shook her head.

"No," she said. Her hand prepared to close the door.

Bishop said:

"I heard from someone that Mrs. Martin lived here. At 24a Delford Lane."

He seemed puzzled, even worried.

"No."

At a loss, and offering his problem to her kindness, he said:

"Joanna's mother—"

The swift eyes flickered and looked away. The woman thought for a moment, then looked at the young man again. There was no softening of glance, speech or feature.

"Bullet Street," she said, "along on the left, at the end here. Number 60. I'm her sister."

Her help had been given simply, roughly and directly. The eyes remained hard; the voice ceased its grating; the lines of reticence were immovable in the set features. But she had helped, since the young man seemed at a loss.

"Thank you," he said, relieved. "I'll go along there now."

She said nothing. He turned for the steps.

"I'm sorry I had to trouble you."

Halfway up the steps he heard:

"That's all right."

He reached the street.

Along to the end, and on the left, he found Number 60 Bullet Street. There was no basement to this house. Had there been a basement, the tall scraggy honeycomb of bricks would surely have plunged into it, after the weathers and the slam of doors and the tramp of feet and the bombs. It was a dirty, tired house.

The front door was wide open, as if someone had felt a sudden but cumulative revulsion of those naked stairboards, the wallpaper that hung in peeling strips from the decaying plaster, the mahogany stand that leaned with an inert agony beneath the gross burden of the plant-pot, with its treasure of withered leaves—as if someone had felt the sudden need of air and sunlight, and the easy gentleness of natural scenes—a hill, a tree, a stream—as if someone had started up and run from the house with feet desperate for distance alone.

The hall was empty; the stairs were silent; the passage that flanked the banisters ran deep into the gloom and promised to lead nowhere less hideous than here.

The young man on the top step looked for a bell or a knocker; there was neither. He raised his hand to rap at the blistered panels of the door, and remained with his hand lifted as the voice behind him said:

"What you want?"

He turned and saw a man standing on the pavement, squinting up at him, his eyes drilling upwards from a bed of stubbled flesh.

"I'm looking for Mrs. Martin."

"'Ow d'you know she lives 'ere?"

"Her sister told me."

"You been to 'er sister's then?"

"Yes. I've just come from there."

"Goin' the long way about it, ain't you? She'll be at the *Gunner*'s."

Bishop went down the steps to the pavement.

"Thanks," he said.

The *Gunner's Arms* was at the end of the street. He had already passed it. He went into the public bar.

"Yes, love?"

"Hallo," he said. "I'd like a bitter."

The woman's lean hand pulled at the beer engine. He looked around him. Four men played darts near the window. A bus conductor with his face tanned from last week-end on his allotment sat on a stool, a fiber attaché-case near his feet.

"There y'are, love."

He paid. He said:

"I heard I could find Mrs. Martin here."

The woman turned her head.

"O'ver there," she said.

He went across to the corner of the room. The girl lifted her face, surprised to see him standing over her. She was perhaps twenty-two, with a cheap neat dress and sloppy shoes; her eyes were blank.

"Please excuse me," he said quietly. "I'm trying to find Mrs. Martin. Joanna's mother. Yours is the same name, isn't it?"

"That's right."

She stared up at him, with honest, unwavering, utterly blank eyes. Nothing seemed to have registered in her mind.

"You must be Joanna's sister."

"She never had a sister."

He tried again.

"Her brother's wife, then. Mrs. Martin."

The eyes did not change.

"That's right."

Bishop said "Ah" and sat down on the bench. Her glass was more than half full. He said: "Did you know Joanna?"

"Yes."

"I didn't know Joanna," he said reflectively. "But I knew Speight." He took some of his beer. "He was a rum devil."

She said nothing.

A man got a double-three and a grunt of acclaim went up in unison from the three other players. They moved towards the bar. Bishop said to the girl:

"Of course you know he's got out."

"Yes."

She drank, setting the glass down again on her crossed knee and holding it, looking past Bishop to the dart players.

Bishop said: "Did you ever see anything of him?"

"Who?"

Softly and fiercely he said:

"The murderer."

Her thin pale face remained expressionless. She did not look away from the dart players. He thought she wouldn't have looked away from the dart players even if his soft, fierce whisper had been a fiendish yell.

"No," she said.

He drew in a sustaining breath and said:

"I'd like to get you a drink. What'll you have?"

"Gin," she said swiftly, without looking at him.

He got up cheerfully. He had found the key. He brought it to her.

"Cheer-o," she said.

"Cheer-o."

"There are some stories," he said easily, "about Joanna's murder that some people could tell, if they chose. Aren't I right?"

She finished her gin at the second bite and looked at him.

"You the Press?"

He said: "There are stories about that tragedy that even the Press couldn't print."

"I don't know about that, I'm sure."

Color was coming into the face. Expression was creeping into the voice. He thought after six gins the woman would live again. He fetched another for her, and a beer for himself.

"It's not Joanna I'm so interested in," he said. "Nobody can do anything for that poor kid."

He felt the physical shock of her laugh. It came out in a sudden whinny. One of the dart players turned his head and grinned at her.

"Poor kid," she said to Bishop. "*That* bitch!"

Bishop sipped his beer.

Putting gin into Mrs. Martin was like putting petrol into a car.

"Not that I wish to speak ill of the dead," she said, "I'm sure." She finished her short, sharp whinny on a titter and got back to the serious business of her glass.

Bishop couldn't go wrong now. He said:

"Oh, Joanna was a decent enough sort. I think a lot of people misjudged her, you know."

"Joanna Martin," said Mrs. Martin deliberately, "was born to be murdered. All I'm saying is that I think she was damned clever to last as long as she did without getting herself cut up and thrown to the moggies."

After he had waited to hear if she had anything to add to her sister-in-law's obituary, Bishop asked her:

"Mervyn Speight wasn't the only one who didn't seem to get on with her, then?"

"He was the one with guts."

"The others hadn't got guts?"

"Nobody's got guts," she said, and gave a slight giggle, and looked into her glass. "Or there'd be a bloody revo-revolution, woul'n't there, see?"

"Let's not talk about politics."

"'T'isn' politics, i's revolution, an' when I say bloody revolution I mean blood'n-gutsy an' not jus' swearin'—you ought to hear Charlie, on about revo-revolution—Charlie says—"

"Charlie's your husband?"

She swiveled a wide-eyed stare.

"You don't think I'm not married?"

"Joanna knew a lot of men, didn't she?"

"Plenty. Charlie spent a lot of his time tryin' to keep her out of trouble, but—"

"Did she know a man called Tasman?"

"Who?"

"Tasman." He spelt it for her.

"I dunno."

"Have you ever heard the name?"

"It's a queer one, in' it?"

"D'you remember the names of any of the men she went about with?"

"I don' think you're the Press. You from the p'lice or—"

"Think of their names. I'll get you another gin. A big double gin. Bargain?"

She sulked over the dregs of her glass until he returned from the bar. The barmaid had given him a straight look. The dart players were also looking at him. The bus conductor had gone out.

Mrs. Martin accepted her replenishment with an attempt at mustered dignity.

"Just gettin' me drunk, you are, so's I'll shoot me mouth off."

Bishop sat down beside her and said quickly:

"A pound a name. Roll, bowl or pitch, and nothing barred."

"Who the hell *are* you?"

"Your best customer."

She sulked for a minute or two and drank half her gin and then said:

"There was one called Emmerson. Had a car an' some money. She tried to get too much."

"What was her exact line?"

She turned a brassy laugh on him.

"'Ow long you been alive?"

"All right," he said. "Emmerson. Tall man? Young one?"

"Little bloke with glasses an'—"

"Think of another one."

"Do I get me—"

"Yes, when we leave here. Another name?"

"Jimmy Brown," she said pertly. "He was—"

"Don't make them up."

Her head swung again.

"How d'you know if I make 'em up or not. I'd like to—"

"I just know. Go on—another name, a real one."

A round of laughter went up from the dart players. They weren't looking this way. The barmaid was giggling with them and serving a big fat man who had come in.

"A man she called Sidney," said Mrs. Martin, smouldering over her gin.

"Sidney who?"

"I dunno. She was cagey. He was a flash sort, smoked cigars. He tried to get me once an' I smacked his chops f'r 'im, quick as you like—"

"Small man?"

"Cocky little rat, 'e was, wore rings an'—"

"I'll buy him. Next?"

"Next?"

"Another name."

"Speight."

"You said you didn't know Speight."

"I didn't know all of 'em—she was cagey—"

"Did you ever hear her talk about a man called Speight?"

"Well, 'e killed her, di'n"e?"

"But she never talked about him. Did she? I'll buy this one, anyway, but I want the truth."

"I can't say as I'm sure I heard 'er mention 'im, but it only goes to reason—"

"Until you read about the murder and Speight's arrest, you didn't hear his name? Or did you?"

"I don't think I did. You're confusin' me."

"Another name. Think of another name."

She held her head with one hand and closed her eyes.

"I can't think straight. I'm feelin' queer."

"Take your time. There were a lot of men. Any name will do."

"There was the Gent," she said feebly.

He waited. She said nothing.

"Yes, what gent?"

"She called 'im that. The Gent. I never heard what 'is name was, his real name."

"Did you see him? Tall, short, big, small?"

"I dunno. I dunno. I feel queer—"

"The Gent. The Gent. Think about him—"

"A toff, he was. Business-man sort. I feel sick."

"Did she try it on too much with the Gent?"

Sweat filmed her nose. Bishop's eyes did not move from her face.

"I dunno, straight."

He got up.

"Let's go outside."

He took her arm, helping her to put the glass down. It was still half full. As they went out there was a brief silence. The barmaid said nothing as they went. After the swing-door closed, the voices broke out again.

Bishop took the girl's arm and walked her slowly along, the other way from Bullet Street where she lived. They walked along a wider road where there were no shops and only a few children playing.

The air was fresh, after the tap-room smell.

"Where did the Gent come from?"

"I don't know. He'ad a car."

Most of Joanna's gentlemen seemed to have had cars. Cars and cigars. She'd been quite a digger.

"What age was he?"

She said nothing. She leaned on him heavily, and once or twice her high heels ricked over and he had to help her.

"Middle-aged?" he asked gently.

"Yes, 'e wasn't young. Take me 'ome. Please take me 'ome."

He turned left at the next corner.

"I am. Was he a thin man? Tall?"

She tripped again.

"Big," she said.

He asked her again what sort of man the Gent had been, going over the same questions two or three times. They turned left again, and came into Bullet Street. He walked her to the house and up the steps.

He said: "I've bought the Gent. I'll give you double for anything more you can tell me about him."

She leaned against the door-post, holding her head. Her face was white.

"I dunno," she said. "I dunno."

He said: "Come in and sit down."

She led him into a ground-floor room full of second-hand furniture and the smell of humanity in its worst mood. He made her sit down on a padded arm-chair whose stuffing sprouted like soft fluffy warts.

She stared up at him, her lids sagging, her eyes blank.

"Who're you?" she said without interest.

"Feel all right?"

"Cruel."

"Just sick?"

She nodded.

He said: "Well, you know where everything is. You live here, don't you?"

Again she nodded.

He asked, "Where can I find Joanna's mother?"

138

Her head lolled.

"Said she'd meet me down the pub . . . silly old cow . . . feel so bad, I do."

He hesitated. Mothers were biased about their murdered daughters. If he found Joanna's mother, he would probably learn less than he had from this girl. It could have been a useful mistake.

He'd leave it at that for now.

"When will Charlie be home?" he asked.

"Night," she moaned.

"You'll feel better by then."

He ticked five pound notes into her loose fingers and went to the door.

"What you done t' me?" she said in a sing-song way.

He said: "It does look a bit like that, but we understand, don't we?"

He went out and down into the street.

12th

MOVE

♛ DU VANCET had planned things with an informal intimacy, taking over the American bar at the Cola Club. The lighting was well down; there was no music; the room had been sprayed with something remarkably ably like *Danse de la Lune,* but at seven guineas a flask it was either extravagance or dedeception.

About fifty people were here. Du Vancet disliked crowds and was select: of these fifty, a good thirty would buy. Even at his prices.

There was no persuasion, however, in any direct manner. All round the room there were chairs. You could sit with your drink, and there was ample room for waiters to move about in, replenishing your palate. You need not look at the models as they walked from the flowered archway nearly to the bar, turned, and walked back. You need not even drink; you could just sit and inhale the remarkably *Danse de la Lune*-like air.

Just the same, there was the definite thought in your mind that if you didn't do anything more than sit and inhale, you'd cause a riot—or worse, a hush—when you left. Even if you drank yourself paralytic and raked the parade with enchanted eyes, your departure would create that certain feeling that would meet you again in the next mirror. You had to be here to buy.

Du Vancet was here himself. A small, wax-polished, mid-European with bottomless eyes and reversible hormones, he drifted ethereally, like a dove seeking its lost soul among a cloister of dreams. He usually cleared fifteen hundred guineas a show.

This one had already started. The girls were walking on, willowing down from the arch of flowers, glancing with fauns' eyes left and right, swirling in a filmy vortex of silk and gliding back to their enchanted bower with the perfumed air seeming to waft them along and their feet definitely killing them.

Rex Willison was saying:

"That's how Rasputin must have selected his slave-girls. Them was the days."

Thelma made a note of an off-the-shoulder cocktailer in sequined black. She was feeling the strain of the night, and the lack of sleep. The heavy perfume in the air, the soft lighting, the murmur of voices, the hypnotic movement of the models gave her a sensation of unreality, of a dream trapped in a bottle, a dream that would at any moment become a nightmare—heated, restless, unfolding without mercy.

The flowers would shrivel to macabre shapes, their whorls of petals transformed to cold, dead ears struck off from dying heads; the girls would glide like ghosts fleeing from a torture bed, their smiles fixed in the agony of death without end, dance without music, world without life.

"Oh, hello Maurice."

She turned her head, her lids lifting swiftly.

Willison moved his chair, making room.

Jerrold sat down quietly, at pains not, to cause an interruption.

"Thought I'd come along," he murmured softly.

Thelma smiled and turned her head again as another model left the archway, moving towards them.

Jerrold watched the parade for fifteen minutes, saying nothing. Thelma's face was pale; he had noted it. Faint blue rings had formed below her eyes, and they were apparent despite her make-up; he did not miss them. The fingers of her left hand were restless against the note book, and her shorthand was jerky with the effort of over-control; this did not escape him.

When the show broke up, Jerrold took his fashion writer and his photographer to the bar at the end of the room. He ordered drinks and then turned his back very slightly on Willison, lowering his voice.

"All right, Thelma?"

She nodded, smiling.

"Of course. Why did you come up?"

He shrugged, giving her a cigarette, waving the case to Willison, who shook his head. Willison was a specialist; just now he was drinking.

Jerrold murmured: "I don't know. Just a feeling." He looked at her directly. "It's possible that you run a certain risk."

She sipped her sherry.

"Don't worry about me, Maurice. You ought to be sitting on your lawn, watching Mick and Jonathan mowing it. You didn't come up only because you were worried about me?"

"No I—had a few things to see to at the office." He felt suddenly a little foolish from her point of view, coming up to town off the record because he was worried about her. She looked pale, and her eyes showed strain; but she wasn't breaking up. He was worried about other things, too, but they wouldn't have got him up to London. He had confidence.

He stood with his feet slightly astride, his large head held forward a fraction as he drank. He looked like the biggest buyer here; the fact was that he was the biggest seller—of du Vancet's creations. Gloria del Ray was the middle-man, the one with a flair for words. This show would be run again, in the Miller-Group magazine; the models would parade again, this time down the glossy pages of *Venus*.

Jerrold said quietly:

"Has he tried to reach you?"

She looked quickly at her cigarette.

"By phone, yes."

He watched her face.

"You've talked to him?"

"No."

He noticed vaguely the strong man who was standing at the bar behind Thelma. Jerrold looked critically and by habit at the young man's suit, and priced it at fifty guineas.

Thelma said:

"I'm covering the hats at Forsyth's just after lunch. Do you want sketches or pictures?"

He thought of Mervyn Speight, his hand dialling at a telephone.

"Pictures. Don't you think?"

"Yes. I'll take Rex along."

The young man turned and said: "Hello."

Thelma looked round.

"Oh, hello."

She introduced them, Maurice Jerrold, her editor-in-chief, Hugo Bishop, a friend of hers.

Jerrold said: "You've seen the show?"

"Some of it."

"What do you think?"

"There's gold in them thar frills."

Jerrold laughed.

"I like that. I wish we could buy it for *Venus,* but it isn't the angle that pays."

Thelma's glass was empty. Bishop said:

"What would you like?"

"Sherry, please. Dry."

"And you, Mr. Jerrold?"

"Thanks. I'd like gin and French."

Willison moved into the group. He was a specialist, and this seemed to be Miller-Group's ride. Jerrold said:

"Hugo Bishop, a friend of Thelma's. Rex Willison, our chief photographer."

They nodded.

Willison said: "What'll you have?"

"You're just too late."

"All right. I'll have Scotch."

Bishop added it to the order. Jerrold said:

"I've seen you before, Mr. Bishop. Recently."

"Yes?"

"I can't place just where. Unless it was in an antique shop, about a week ago?"

Bishop passed Thelma her drink.

"That could be," he said. "But, in fact, that isn't an antique shop. It's my motor-car."

Jerrold looked puzzled. Thelma smiled.

"He has a very old Rolls-Royce, Maurice. But beautifully preserved."

Willison picked up his Scotch.

"Cheers."

They all drank. Bishop said:

"I've just been checking up on Joanna Martin."

Willison jerked a glance upwards from his glass and found himself looking into Bishop's rather vague grey eyes.

Jerrold frowned, drawing his head back and looking at Bishop.

Thelma's expression did not change. Willison said:

"I'm sorry. I must have missed some of the conversation." He lifted his glass again, but his eyes did not leave Bishop.

"Apparently she was an unpleasant little girl," Bishop said easily. "I've been talking to her sister-in-law."

After a slight pause Willison said:

"And has her sister-in-law been talking to you?" Bishop looked at him.

"She wasn't uninformative."

Thelma was finishing her sherry too quickly for her palate to enjoy it. Jerrold was taking out a cigarette-holder, and fitting into it his already half-burned cigarette, seemingly as an after-thought. It occupied his hands.

"Are you doing a write-up?" Willison asked Bishop.

"No, I just thought that as Mervyn Speight was larking about in London, it might be interesting to open up old history." He looked at Thelma, his eyes a little amused. "Perhaps I take a morbid pleasure in other people's tragedies."

She looked away, putting her empty glass on to the bar.

"I must go. My chief's a slave-driver."

Jerrold smiled.

"But I like my slaves to be plump. Are you free for lunch?"

"I am."

"May I?"

"I'd love it."

They left together; Bishop and Willison remained at the bar, Willison said:

"I don't know why you're interested in the Joanna Martin affair. It's not my business. But I'm interested in it because I took the first photographs in Ludgate Hill."

"Yes?"

"I was on an impromptu assignment for a syndicate. Rush job, of course."

"Of course. Murder seldom happens slowly, does it?"

"I took some good pictures. The ruins. X marks the spot. Speight being bundled into the Maria. More of Speight—closeups, after the trial. A murderer has a higher price on his face after he's officially opened to the public by the judge's pronouncement. I've one or two that couldn't be printed. One always has. You might like to see them some time."

"I'd like to very much."

Willison finished his drink. Bishop said:

"Still on Scotch?"

"No-no, this is mine."

He ordered a repeat and turned back to Bishop, lighting a cigarette.

"You know Thelma long?"

"Some time," Bishop said.

"She's a nice kid. Tasman's a lucky brigand."

"I haven't met him."

"Bit of a bore, I suppose. Drinks petrol and talks exhaustively about his job. But damned clever at it."

"Backroom boy."

Willison nodded.

"Yes. He's down in Bristol at the moment; bit of a shame, leaving a girl like Thelma on the hat stand. I wouldn't."

"No. But he'll be coming back."

Willison grinned.

"Your point." He took his drink and halved it smoothly.

Bishop thought it was time he went. Nearly everyone had gone—Jerrold, Thelma, her police-shadow and most of the buyers she had mingled with.

This morning had been successful in one of two ways; but you had to know when to stop.

He finished his sherry.

Willison said:

"Any time you want to see those pictures, let me know. You can always find me at Miller-Group."

"I'll remember that."

Bishop looked in at one of the telephone boxes on his way out. His number was in.

"Good morning, Frederick."

Frisnay said: "I was hoping you'd ring."

"So you have two wishes left. You must choose carefully, or the Robber Baron will—"

"Oh, you're in that mood."

"Now, don't be so hasty, Frederick. I'm about to offer you lunch—"

"I don't want to eat. I want to talk."

"You want to talk—I want to eat. We'll talk over lunch. Solomon would've said that. Say, in fifteen minutes at Chiang's—"

"I can't make it—"

"You'll wish you had—"

"You think you can just ring me up and—"

"Give me the Yard and I'll take a mile. See you at Chiang's."

He left the telephone box.

Saturday morning had gone off with a bang. By tonight there'd be the recoil. Meantime, he felt like some crispy noodles. Was that so crazy?

13th

MOVE

FRISNAY SAT with his hands folded on the table and his favorite sprig of hair sticking up from the crown, like a cross parrot's poll. He had tried water, brilliantine, Gleemcreem, bay-rum and spirit-gum. Now he just let it stick up.

Bishop said:

"Fried soft noodle, lobster and bean-shoots, sweet-and-sour, mushrooms and pancake roll."

The waiter jotted.

"Fried rice," Frisnay said.

"And fried rice," Bishop said.

"Flied lice," the waiter said, and went away.

Frisnay said:

"You must have been mistaken. Or we'd have got him."

"It ain't necessarily so. Perhaps you didn't try hard enough."

"Possibly we didn't," said Frisnay. "All we had were thirty specials, twelve patrol-cars and half a dozen late-duty men, apart from the normal contingent in that area. Perhaps I should have called in a pixie with X-ray eyes." He looked inertly at the soya sauce. "The whole team was on the spot within six minutes of your phone call."

Bishop shrugged, looking absently at a nice little snub-nosed Malay girl using chopsticks in a corner of the restaurant. He said:

"Just bad luck, then. It was Speight I saw. He couldn't have been more than six minutes from Ludgate Hill when your men moved in. Are they still checking?"

Frisnay nodded.

"Hotels, boarding-houses, service-rooms—the routine drill. No go. What makes you so certain it was Speight you saw? Have you ever seen him before?"

"No."

Frisnay moved his hands slightly.

"But I talked to him," Bishop said.

"On the phone?"

"On the bombed-site."

Frisnay's eyes flickered. He said:

"You *talked* to him."

"That's right."

"You were as close as that."

"As that."

Frisnay looked at the cloth.

"And you couldn't nab him."

"If I could have nabbed him, I wouldn't have got you to call out the heavy mob."

"Was he armed?"

"No. Or, if he was, he was shy about it."

"What did you talk about?"

"Oh, this and that. Murder, and things."

Frisnay immoblized his face and said:

"Yes?"

Bishop nodded absently.

"Yes."

A resigned expression crept across Frisnay's face. He wanted to tell Bishop that he couldn't leave the subject in the air. He felt that if he told Bishop, Bishop would. Just out of cussedness. He'd asked Frisnay to lunch because he wanted something—a name, a number, a lead, a clue—something the Yard might be able to give him. Well, he'd have to dig for it, he couldn't just ask outright.

"I thought we came here to talk," Frisnay said.

Bishop sat back in his chair as the bowls began arriving. "No," he said. "I wanted to eat. It was you who wanted to talk. Remember?"

"I'm bad at monologues," Frisnay said gloomily.

Bishop gave a quick sigh.

"Then I'll pass the time of the day. I've just spent a pleasing half-hour watching a fashion show.

The woman beautiful is never more fascinating than when she's been got up by Paris to look like a broomstick, a left-angled parallelogram or a schizophrenic pterodactyl. There was one model wearing plastic-elastic plackets with *motif* of spread-eagled pansies—"

"Have some fried rice," Frisnay said. "It muffles the voice."

Bishop helped himself.

"I met Mrs Speight there," he said smoothly.

Frisnay moved the sweet-and-sour nearer his host.

"Yes?" he said.

"Yes. And Maurice Jerrold, her chief. And Rex Willison, her photographer. They all seemed politely interested."

"In what?"

"My mentioning that I'd just been chatting with Joanna Martin's sister-in-law."

Frisnay squirted the soya sauce over his bean-shoots and passed the bottle.

He said: "Now we're beginning to talk."

"You're wrong. Now we're beginning to eat."

Little more was said for half an hour; when the li-chee came, talking was resumed. Both men felt more at ease with life on a full stomach. Bishop put a fruit in his spoon and said:

"I phoned your office, earlier this morning. They said you were out. I lavished blandishments upon your doughty sergeant, and learned you'd gone to Broadmoor."

"I had."

"Interesting?"

"Not very."

"But slightly?"

Frisnay said: "I had a talk with the Medical Superintendent. He tried to be helpful, of course. There just wasn't anything to give me a clue."

"Clue to what?"

"To where Speight's hiding up. I think frankly that he'll show himself once too often and we'll grab him long before we can work out where his nest is."

Frisnay was not looking at Bishop. Bishop looked at Frisnay and said:

"Now don't try to pull the wool over your auntie's tear-dimmed eyes."

"If you choose to think I am—"

"I don't choose. It just hits me smack in my face. You're not going to sit back on this break and trust in the Lord. It's not your temperament and not your orders. Speight could rub out another life, at any minute. His crime appeared to have a sex-motive. He's been cooped up, a celibate for two years. Now he's loose in London among an eight-million population and tonight it'll be dark again."

He finished his li-chee and added:

"You want Speight like a nigger wants salt. And you want him before dark. If I thought for an instant there was anything more I could do to help, I'd tell you and try to do it. As I did last night, however fruitlessly. So please don't think I'm playing touched-you-last, much as I enjoy tugging your scraggy leg."

He ordered coffee. When the waiter had gone, he added: "I hope you can say the same."

Frisnay said mildly: "I'm not holding anything back, even for official reasons. The Med-Super said Speight showed slight tendencies towards the manic-depressive—"

"So would I, in Broadmoor."

"Quite. He stressed the word 'slight.' But a manic-depressive can boil over, however slight the bias is from normal."

"Whatever 'normal' means," said Bishop. "Half the world's cuckoo these days. The other half's running to psychoanalysts—sure sign they want their heads tested. If the Med-Super had said Speight was murderously manic-depressive, that'd be different."

Slowly Frisnay said: "He was found guilty but insane."

"I'm not saying he isn't insane, Freddie. But there are degrees."

"I don't follow."

Frisnay's tone was steady. Bishop looked at him for an instant, weighed the ethics and the incumbencies of their two positions—that of the civilian and the civil servant—and decided to play for prudence. They had known each other a very long time; too well to dispense with with tact. Frisnay was a policeman. There were things you could not tell policemen, and there were things you could not expect them to tell you.

Already Bishop had implied more than he would have declared directly.

He said:

"I'm not sure of my ground. When I've gone over it, I might be able to say something useful. I hope so. People are edgy all the time Speight's loose."

Frisnay stirred his coffee, and did not look up until Bishop asked:

"Did they tell you anything more about Speight, at Broadmoor?"

"A few things. He tried to escape about a month after he was sent there."

Bishop toyed with his spoon.

"Is that unusual?"

"Yes. But not remarkable. Some of them do, until they resign themselves."

"To the trees . . . "

"M'm?"

"Nothing. Did he ever try to cut a vein, or anything?"

"No."

"Why did he try to escape?"

Frisnay gave a thin smile.

"Probably he didn't feel an explanation was needed."

"There could have been several reasons, apart from just wanting to be free."

"Can you suggest some?"

"To see his wife."

Frisnay said: "There wasn't all that love lost between them, from what I can glean. And, anyway, she'd gone abroad."

"Would he have known that?"

"Yes, he was told."

"Italy isn't far, and this country would have been too hot for him if he'd got free."

Frisnay looked at him steadily.

"Maybe you're trying to sell me that reason. Hugo. I don't think it's worth buying, at this stage. Speight's really made it, this time. You think it's still just to see his wife?"

"Or to kill her."

"He'd have got her by now. He's been hanging about, wasting his time—the precious dark hours. Or so you tell me."

Bishop didn't even rise to it. He said:

"Yes, that's true. I don't like the reason I'm trying to sell you, either. I've others—all round ones, no rubbish. For instance, he lost his memory when his head was hit by his fall into the cellars. He might be trying to find it."

"It came back, within a month. I've seen the medical reports. I'm satisfied."

Bishop sipped his coffee. After a while he said: "I don't quite see how they can be certain that *all* his memory came back. Suppose there were something for him to remember that they didn't even know about? Something he knew was there, all the time, right in the background. Something he knew he *must* remember—without even realizing why it was important that he must—"

"Straighten up and fly right," Frisnay said.

Bishop frowned, trying—even as he tried to tell Frisnay—to explain to himself what was forming in his mind.

Frisnay's level voice sounded aslant across his conjectures. He heard only the general meaning of the words:

"I believe you really met Speight on the bombed-site. I don't believe he went there for any reason other than the well-known unexplainable urge that makes a criminal return to the scene."

"It's not unexplainable—especially for a man with manic-depressive tendencies. It would be a form of boasting, wouldn't it?"

Frisnay said: "That fits in. Speight is proud of what he did."

Bishop looked at him curiously.

"Proud?"

"He kept news-cuttings about the murder, and the full reports of his trial. He was headline stuff for a day or two. Few things swell a man's ego so much as a capital trial. It's a very fierce spotlight and the greater part of the audience are women. The joys of exhibitionism—and murderers are prime egomaniacs—often make up for the fear of death."

"Which seldom occurs to them, I imagine."

Frisnay nodded. "They're nearly always sure of getting off. Hanging can't happen to *them*."

"These news-cuttings. They were found on him?"

"He'd hidden them in a cistern-ball. Apart from being rolled up, they were well-thumbed. He must have read them almost every day—"

"Committing them to memory?"

Frisnay blanked his expression again. They were touching the same subject that had been hinted at a few moments ago. Even if their thoughts lay parallel, they had to think them in their own way, individually; unless the idea got too big and had to burst. Officially.

"Not so much committing them to memory," Frisnay's tone edged cautiously round the words, "As simply enjoying them. Reliving the glamorous period when he was in the headlines."

"Trying to recapture memory, then." Bishop was fighting back as gently as his friend. "Trying to recapture *all* of it."

"We have our several views, Hugo."

After a brief silence Bishop said:

"Check." He finished his coffee and signalled for his bill. "Anything else turn up at Broadmoor?"

"Just general reports. Speight was an artist, as you know. Still is. He's done a lot of good work at the institution. Most of the pictures on the reading-room walls are his."

Bishop paid the bill, listening carefully as they strolled out of Chiang's.

"He also made a series of sketches," said Frisnay. "Some of them he left around, and didn't make any effort to hide. Others were found in various places; and when he was questioned he shut up hard, apart from saying they were a subject for practice."

Bishop climbed behind the wheel of his parked car, filling his pipe as Frisnay got in beside him and slammed the door. Bishop said:

"All portraits?"

"Yes. All of the same man." He glanced at Bishop. "How did you know they were portraits? Did Speight say anything about them?"

"No." Bishop lit his pipe and the smoke went trailing through the driving window, dispersing in the sunshine. He started the engine. "But he was good enough to let me see one."

"A sketch?"

"Yes. Probably one of the series. Would you imagine?"

Frisnay sat back with his arms folded, gazing through the windscreen as the Rolls-Royce moved into the traffic flow.

"What," he asked, "was it like?"

"A man's face took up most of the picture. A face not easy to describe. But the expression was violently sketched."

"Of what?"

"Hate. Fear. Maybe both, a mixture. It was bestial and it was extreme; say, something like the expression would be of someone who'd become completely animal, if only for a moment. Someone in a spot, an appalling spot."

Frisnay said nothing for a time. Then:

"Think it might have been an abstract projection of his own personality? A killer, caught?"

"He's never seen himself in that role." Bishop's head turned slightly and he glanced at the inspector. "According to your ideas, he thinks of himself as the hell of a feller, in between being depressive."

"But you think he's more like the picture, I mean as he regards himself?"

"Oh, my dear Freddie, let's not blind ourselves deliberately to the obvious!"

Bishop's voice had cut sharply in the confined space of the car's interior. He had not meant to lose control.

Frisnay's eyes did not leave the traffic scene as the car rounded Eros. He did not turn his head. He did not speak. Bishop said:

"Sorry. What I mean is, that it's pretty clear the portrait is of someone else. Unless we try to hang on to a conviction that's becoming weaker every minute, the way I see it."

He drove more quickly down Coventry Street and nosed the saloon towards Trafalgar Square.

"You know," he went on evenly, "what I'm talking about, and what I'm getting at. But you can pretend not to understand—in fact you've just got to, at this stage, because of your job and your position. That's all right, but there's nothing against my saying a little more: just a little. I think Speight had a damned good reason for breaking out. I don't think it was to see his wife. Or to go to the pictures. Or even to visit the scene of his crime and gloat over the memory."

He span the wheel, selected a gap between a bus and a news van, and slid into it neatly with a split-second caress of the brakes.

"I think Speight got loose to find someone. The face in the sketch. He doesn't know his name, or where he is. He believes he's in London, though. We suspect—but only I can admit it—why he's got to find that face. If we're right, something very big has got to blow up."

Frisnay said quietly:

"Speight is insane. He was certified and committed to a lunatic asylum. Let's not be too logical—about an idea in a madman's mind."

The car whispered down Whitehall and soon turned left. Bishop said:

"You go on looking for Speight. I've spent the day looking for the face in the sketch. And I've found him. If he leads me to Speight, I'll let you know."

For the first time in minutes, Frisnay looked at him in the eyes, as he got out of the car. They were outside the Yard. A constable was walking up slowly to move the car on; then he recognized the inspector. Frisnay said:

"You've seen the face in the sketch?"

"That's right, Freddie. Don't let it worry your little head for the moment, though. I'll ring you this evening."

Frisnay hesitated, then nodded.

"Do."

He turned away, pausing to call back:

"Thanks for the lunch."

"It was worth it," called Bishop, and put the gears into reverse.

Frisnay walked up to his office, sat down behind the desk, and got his sergeant in.

"Baxter, I'm bothered."

"Yes, sir?"

Sergeant Baxter gave him a cigarette. When it was burning, Frisnay said:

"Something very awkward seems to be coming up in the Speight affair. It might not happen. If it does, It'll go up from this office like a rocket, and catch the Assistant-Commissioner plumb in the rump."

Sergeant Baxter's expression did not alter on his lean, pale face. It was the only expression he had, and he used it for everything.

"I want to talk it over with you," his chief said slowly, "but strictly off the record. And not a word to Bessie."

"No, Sir."

"It's going to be tricky to handle, if it's true. If it isn't true and if we give anyone so much as a smell that we've even discussed it as a possibility, we'll get the chopper. All right?"

"All right sir."

Frisnay began talking.

14th

MOVE

♛ "IT MUST be wonderful," said Caprice. Her thin hand applied the cream pack in layers, embalming the client's face. "I'd have a try, but my figure's wrong. Legs too thick—not enough bust . . . "

"I shouldn't worry," the client said. She wished the girl would stop. Stop gabbling and finish the pack, go away, go silently away. "It might seem wonderful to wear a dozen du Vancet dresses in a day, but the work's terribly hard."

"Oh," said Caprice, "I like hard work."

"It's more than hard work. Constantly lifting the arms to get in and out of dresses strains the whole torso. Doctors say that models should take intervals of other work. It never happens, if a girl's got the figure. But by thirty her face begins to show the strain. And varicose veins have started. It's not worth it, except for the glamour; and that's less than skin-deep."

Caprice stood back, applied the eye-pads and adjusted the *crêpe* bandeau.

"Perhaps I'll be a fashion writer," she said. She was very young; about nineteen. She still had centuries in which to be simply everything.

"You're a beautician," the client murmured under the face-pack. "You work on living material. I'd settle for that."

Caprice adjusted the long chair so that her living material lay at ease.

"Perhaps I will, then," she said quietly. She moved to the lamp switches. "Comify, madam?"

"Yes, thank you, Caprice."

The switch clicked. Under their moist pads, the client's eyes reacted, and a sunburst of gold came against the sudden darkness, flaring under her eyelids. Her lips moved slightly beneath the stiffening mask.

"I must leave by five."

Caprice went to the door of the cubicle.

"I won't forget, madam."

The client heard the door open, the click of the girl's footstep on the parquet of the corridor, the door close, the footsteps again more faintly, then silence became almost total. Very softly and from a long distance the sound came of a massage vibrator, and of a foam-bath filling up;

and someone was having her face slapped, and paying the earth for it.

Against the client's eyelids the sunburst was fading, fading and changing, usurped momentarily by the swirl of violet specks that swarmed through the dark like a cosmic nebula. She could hear the beat of her heart, her quiet breath.

The cream had stiffened on her face, tautening the skin. This was how it would be if a corpse newly dead could go on feeling. The dying away of the nerve-light, the shrinking of the facial skin; but there would be no heart-beat, nor sound of breath.

She shook the macabre thought from her mind, and remembered Hugo Bishop, and wondered how he had known where he could find her, at the du Vancet snow. Before he had left her this morning, she had not told him she would be there.

He might possibly have telephoned the office. Constance, on the week-end shift, would have been able to tell him. But that wouldn't have been his way of finding out. She had known him only for an hour or two last night, and a few minutes this morning when he had woken her with tea; but she felt she knew him deeply, without even knowing who he really was, or why he had come to help her.

His explanation had been thin; yet there was nothing about him that suggested police procedure. Enquiry agents did not run old-fashioned

Rolls-Royces nor live in Chelsea.

Hugo Bishop was an enigma, at once mysterious and open; unfathomable and friendly; odd and ordinary. Her sole certain impression of him was that she could trust him completely; but this was merely intuitive.

He had not told her what he had heard when he had answered her telephone last night. The receiver had been pressed closely to his ear, and she had heard no voice from the other end of the wire. She had caught the sound of the dialling-tone when he had replaced the phone, but that told her nothing, except that the caller had rung off.

By his silence he had implied it was Mervyn. But it might have been Miss Gorringe, sending him a wordless signal, prearranged. Turning wearily into bed, she had been certain it was Mervyn who had telephoned; and Bishop's unfamiliar voice had scared him off the line. She could not have gone to bed, could surely not have slept as quickly and as dreamlessly as she had, if she had been alone in the flat; nor even, perhaps, if her companion in the next room had been anyone except Bishop, whom she so strangely trusted.

Voices reached her now, a jumble of talk from a cubicle not far away. She lay supine, her mind's attention alternating between this real moment and memory—the hum of the vibrator, the sound of water gushing into the foam-bath. . . . Hugo

Bishop, his ear to the telephone . . . the voices from the nearby cubicle. . . . Mervyn, dialling her number from a call box perhaps five miles away, or perhaps the one on the corner of Thames Gardens . . . voices, and the steady hum . . . if you need help, telephone Bishop . . . the drowsy humming . . . the soft *burr-burr* of the telephone in Hugo's hand . . . the voices. . . .

The door of this cubicle opened.

Her eyelids flickered, and remembered they could not lift, under the astringent pads. The alternating of her mind had stopped; she was switched to the real moment around her. She felt drowsy, or as if she had just been dozing off.

Her lips moved, the words distorted by the mask.

"What time is it, Caprice?"

A small sound came; the movement of Caprice, not far from the doorway.

"Have I dozed off?" asked Thelma.

She lay, waiting for an answer, but no one spoke.

"Caprice!"

There came no reply, save for the sound of someone moving in the cubicle, and the sound of their heavy breathing.

Thelma lay inert, as though she had fainted here in the chair, fainted of fear. Caprice had not answered her, because she was not in here. Someone was in here, within touching distance of the chair. It was not Caprice. She would have answered at once.

The chair was adjusted almost to the horizontal. Thelma lay in it, masked and blinded, and had not the strength to move, even to move her hand, even to call out, even to scream. Her throat was blocked with the slow, choking panic.

Beneath the stiffened mask sweat was springing from the pores of her face and her scalp was crawling.

Of all the places where he might have succeeded in finding her, she had not expected him here. But he was here. She lay exposed to him, defenseless against him, against that hideous strength of his that lay in his stubby hands.

It was not dark in the cubicle. Even through the heavy eye-pads she could discern the flush of light from the open doorway. But this did not help her. Mervyn could not have struck blindly in the dark. He could see her now, in the flush of light.

She felt her lips moving again, trying to form the first letter of his name in a stupid, desperate appeal. She failed.

Movement sounded again in the room; and then a footstep on the floor of the passage. In another second the door had closed, and the footstep was repeated, faintly, from outside.

She jerked a breath and lurched from the chair, the eye-pads dropping as she tugged at the door-handle. The door came open and she leaned into the passage, her arm flying up to stop herself falling. In the sudden glare of the fluorescent lighting her pupils contracted as she stared down the corridor.

Mrs. Carmody was just reaching the swing-doors to the reception room. She pushed them open and went through. They swung behind her.

When Caprice opened them, a moment later, and came into the cubicle passage, she saw her client leaning weakly against the door-post, her brow resting on her hands.

"Mrs. Tasman . . . what's happened?"

Thelma opened her eyes, raising her head. Her masked face was turned towards Caprice and for an instant the eyes carried neither expression nor recognition. Then they changed.

Her voice, distorted by the face-pack, was almost steady.

"Nothing. Nothing, Caprice."

She went back into the cubicle; when the girl followed she found Mrs. Tasman lying in the chair.

"What time is it?"

"Just a quarter to five, madam."

"Start setting me right, would you?"

The girl's tone was puzzled.

"Yes, of course. I was just coming to see you."

She began removing the mask. Thelma lay with closed eyes. She said:

"I gave myself a silly fright just now. I think I'd dozed off, and then someone came in here.

I thought it was you. When I spoke they didn't answer—"

"It was Mrs. Carmody—she left her gloves in here, I think—"

"Yes, I saw her in the passage. It was stupid of me, but it was queer to lie here and realize someone was in the cubicle—I just had to see who it was."

"Of course, Mrs. Tasman. I shouldn't have liked it myself, I'm sorry you were upset."

"Oh, I wasn't really upset. I just don't understand why Mrs. Carmody didn't say something—"

"I don't suppose she heard you speak to her."

For an instant Thelma didn't understand; then she remembered, Mrs. Carmody was deaf.

She left the *Salon des Fleurs* at a few minutes past five. The treatment, that should have left her looks and mood revitalized, had been counterbalanced by the shock of Mrs. Carmody.

She felt a greater strain now than when she had come here. She had wasted an hour of her day.

15th

MOVE

♛ VERA GORRINGE opened the door, came into the room, and turned to close it, her feet silent on the pile carpet. But she did not close the door.

Her eyes widened and her glance returned to the scene that had stayed her hand on the door, her feet on the carpet, the breath in her throat.

Hugo Bishop was in the room. His body lay prone, with the feet almost together. The right arm was flung out; the left hand was beneath the davenport. His head rested on the carpet, his face turned towards the davenport. His eyes were wide open.

Miss Gorringe drew a breath, gently after the first shock. Beneath the davenport, Bishop's hand moved, and a glass marble came rolling into view.

The Princess Chu Yi-Hsin leapt upon the marble, trapped it with her forepaws and cuffed it across the carpet, frisking after it with the mischievous madness that sometimes come to cats.

Bishop got up.

Miss Gorringe closed the door.

"I thought you were dead," she said.

He observed her.

"No. I was listening for the Redskins. I think they're heading this way, the murderous fiends —you'd better take Cathy to the canyon and wait for the posse—I'll head 'em off with Silver! When you hear shooting—"

"I only mentioned," said Miss Gorringe patiently, "that I thought you were dead. I was not soliciting nitwittery."

The glass marble banged into the wainscoting and Chu Yi-Hsin went thummocking after it with paws spread-eagling.

Bishop watched her, wondering if she found in the marble the same fascination that he found in the Victorian glass paper-weight on his desk. Transparency was beautiful in its own right; the cat was chasing an enigma; a mere depth of light that was strangely tangible.

He lit his pipe.

"Since jesting seems beneath thy mood, thou haughty Ermyntrude, let us turn the tongue to graver theme, and—"

Miss Gorringe made a detour round the cloud of smoke and said:

"Freddie Frisnay is worried, Hugo."

"Oh? He shouldn't be. He's full of noodles, and ought to be feeling smug. I don't understand Frederick at all. He treats good food as an excuse for talking to the people who pay the bill. He gets indigestion as a result."

"He telephoned, just before you came in and started playing marbles."

Miss Gorringe sat down at her writing desk, and opened a drawer.

Bishop shrugged, kicking the marble for Chu Yi-Hsin.

"I dropped him at the Yard only half an hour ago. He can't have got worried again in less than half an hour."

"So he was worried at lunch?"

"Well, a little earnest."

"When he spoke to me on the phone, it sounded as if you'd rattled him."

"I had."

"Was that wise?"

"It was fun."

Vera Gorringe took a folio from the drawer, slapped it on her desk and looked up.

"When you've outgrown your tra-la-la frame of mind, Hugo, I should like to discuss business."

"Business?"

"The Speight case."

"Ah. You're quivering for a report of my latest

findings." He coiled himself comfortably on the davenport and looked at her across the room. "You know what rattled Freddie? I told him I'd seen the face in the portrait."

Miss Gorringe looked him back.

"In Speight's sketch?"

"In that."

"And it is true?"

"There wouldn't have been much point in telling Freddie if it weren't true. I could have told him a lot of things that'd rattle the old devil, but I wasn't out simply to produce an effect."

"You were out to provoke a reaction."

"How well you know me."

"How well I should. So you've really seen the living face."

"The original of the likeness that Speight showed me on the bombed-site. Without the diabolical expression, of course."

"Are you certain you're right?"

"It depends less on my powers of recognition than on Speight's ability to draw. If his portrait is a good one, I've seen the sitter."

"When, Hugo?"

"Today."

Vera Gorringe sat upright, with her smooth hands clasped on the opened folio. She said gently:

"At breakfast, we decided we weren't really looking for Mervyn Speight, but for a reason and a person—the reason for his escape and the

175

person he escaped to find. And probably both are one. The face of the portrait is clearly the face of the person. You've now seen the original. Is this case closing?"

He smiled faintly.

"No."

She relaxed. She said:

"I can stand almost anything, except a good case folding up on us. So you don't know where to find the person again?"

"But I do."

Miss Gorringe sat back in her chair, leveling her gaze.

"Do you know his name?"

"Yes."

"Then I must be wrong. It doesn't seem very important that we've found the person."

"No?"

"If it were, you'd express something."

He got up from the davenport, striking another match for his meerschaum.

"I admire you, Gorry. You've asked me five or six times to tell you who the person is—without actually asking me."

"Obviously you want the enjoyment of having me ask point-blank. You've slipped into your well-worn smug mood, and while that's preferable to the tra-la-la technique, it's still slightly annoying. *Kamerad:* who is the person?"

He shook his head.

"I'm not monkeying about, Gorry. I'm not even

asking you to guess who it is, just to see if you've had the right person in mind. But I'd rather not tell you, that's all. Yet."

She watched him as he paced easily the length of the room, turning and pacing back. Her rather vague and colorless eyes were without expression; but she was thinking, as she watched him, that if he had really seen the face of the portrait, and knew his name, he must have worked hard this morning; and he must be very good. He hadn't had long, since the meeting with Mervyn Speight.

"You see," Bishop said, "I'm thinking of getting a few people together—or arranging that we meet them at a party, this evening. Among others; I hope to introduce you to our person. And I'd rather you didn't know him, when that happens; because by that time he might be a bit suspicious of me. He won't be suspicious of you."

"You'll introduce me as your great-aunt, or someone innocuous?"

He nodded.

"Someone even less familiar than an aunt. A slight acquaintance." He stopped moving, and stood gazing at Chu Yi-Hsin, who had curled up broodily over her marble. "I know you can act, Gorry, but I don't want our man to get the slightest impression that he interests you."

His voice faded off. For fully three minutes he remained staring at the cat, and Miss Gorringe did not break the silence in the room. Where he was traveling, in these minutes, or whom he was seeing and perhaps talking to in his thoughts, she had no idea; but she would have liked to follow the drift of that searching mind.

He looked round at her suddenly.

"All right?"

She nodded.

"I'll settle for that, Hugo. It might be rather interesting for me, trying to pick him out."

"If you do," he said quickly and seriously, "Let me know. And tell me why he's your bet. If we both select the same person—I from his portrait and you from your own line of logic or intuition—that'll really show us we're on the beam."

He began pacing again and dropped a shower of ash over the Princess by mistake, talking on quickly:

"I'm not certain I can fix it—getting these people together and getting you to meet them just at the right moment. But it'll be worth trying. Perhaps by tonight the case might really close. But I've a feeling it won't just fold up."

Miss Gorringe said:

"Even if they find Speight?"

He thought for a while, then said: "If they find him, the case doesn't fold. It opens. So far we're just scratching the surface. But theories are only skin-deep. We'll go on scratching."

"Did you tell Freddie Frisnay you'd seen the face of the portrait?"

"Yes."

"That's what rattled him."

"Partly. He was also feeling a bit mopey about last night. He really believes I talked to Speight in Ludgate Hill; what he finds it hard to believe is that they missed him so easily, although I gave them the signal within moments of leaving Speight."

Miss Gorringe said: "Was Freddie rattled about anything else?"

"Yes. I made an implication at lunch. It nearly choked him."

Bishop's pacing finished behind his desk. He leaned with his back to it, looking out of the bay-window into King's Road. Saturday traffic was moving there, and the pavements were crowded with people buying for the week-end. Mervyn Speight had lived here, in Chelsea, two years ago. His studio had been in Church Street. He knew this scene well. Perhaps, at this moment he was part of it, wandering on his search for the man who had lived in London two years ago. The man in the sketch.

Bishop's pipe had gone out again. He relit it, and thought that Speight would not find that person here today. Somewhere in London, maybe, but not in Chelsea.

He said: "The implication I made, Gorry, was received rather badly by our Frederick. I simply suggested that Mervyn Speight might not have murdered Joanna Martin."

Miss Gorringe did not move behind her desk.

It was smaller than Bishop's, but tidier. It accommodated files, records, indexes, writing-paper and other ordinary equipment; it was not littered, like Bishop's, with chess-pieces, glass paper-weights, ivory miniatures, sheets of swing music, old theater programs, older pipes, ancient curios from Egypt, elastic bands, pipe-cleaners, and out-of-date copies of *The Connoisseur, The Countryman, Autosport* and *London Life*.

Vera Gorringe had once described his enormous limed-oak desk as "insanitary." From behind the more hygienic composure of her own she now looked up at him.

"If you told Freddie that," she said, "I'm not surprised he was rattled. I doubt if the phrase 'miscarriage of justice' is very popular at New Scotland Yard."

"Even less at the Law Courts. But I wouldn't have even implied the idea to Freddie if I didn't take it seriously. He began fighting me, from the first hint."

"Reasonably?"

"To a certain extent. But mainly, I felt, on principle."

Miss Gorringe turned a page of the folio in front of her.

"Rather a shaker, Hugo."

"Yes, isn't it. If there's any sense in my idea, there's a big swing-over. Finding Speight isn't so important anymore, because if he didn't kill Joanna Martin he's not a homicidal maniac—

and his wife is safe, and so are a few hundred thousand girls and young women all over London. That crime suggested strongly a sex-motive. When I talked to Speight last night I tried to see him as the kind of screwball who had that sort of evil in his make-up. I just couldn't fit it in—although it's never easy to discern latent explosive inside a person; most often it's there, but never blows up."

Miss Gorringe looked down the sheet of her folio. He said from across the room:

"Is that the report of the trial?"

"Yes."

"I thought you'd fish that out."

"Of course. Your idea's based on Speight's defense. Isn't it?"

"Oddly enough, no. It began in my mind when I was talking to Joanna's sister-in-law this morning. But his defense makes a solid background. Stop me if I go wrong. In court, Speight claimed that he had been passing the bombed-site in Ludgate Hill, heard the woman in trouble, went to her succor and was knocked unconscious by her assailant. That was his explanation for his being found in the ruined cellar a few yards from Joanna's body. Yes?"

"Yes."

"And his inability to remember a single detail about the alleged assailant was explained by temporary and partial loss of memory caused by the knock-out-blow."

181

He turned from the window and sat down slowly in the chair behind the desk, gazing again at the Siamese, who slept with her marble, her head still decorated with pipe ash.

"Let's face it," he said: "the defense had got a pretty thin story to put across. The prosecution had an easy job, in the main: Speight possessed a quick temper that had already put his marriage in jeopardy—and although the defense raised an immediate objection, the damage was done. But more important: why couldn't he recall the assailant in any sort of detail—on this moonlit night and in this lamplit spot—and yet could recall going to the girl's help and meeting the assailant's opposition? And why was the injury to his head so compatible with sudden contact with a hard, rough surface such as masonry, when he claimed to have been knocked unconscious by a blow?"

Miss Gorringe said:

"Because the man hit him with a stone."

"Of course. He had to . . . if the defense was going to stand up at all. As it was, the defense began tottering. The best it could do was to say that either Speight spoke the truth, or he was insane at the time of the murder, which was apparently motiveless as it concerned *him*. The prosecution accepted the surrender, declined to fight the suggested pleas of insanity, and left it to the jury. After the judge's summing-up, there wasn't any question as to what the jury should bring in."

"You believe they could have hanged Speight, without the insanity plea?"

Bishop shook his head.

"Thin though the defense was, I don't think so. Evidence was entirely circumstantial, and there was a doubt. But I don't think the country would have stood for an acquittal. There was only one compromise, and it was made."

Miss Gorringe turned a dozen sheets of the folio. She said:

"The Press seemed to be satisfied."

"The Press was told to be satisfied."

He raked out the ash from his pipe and left the bowl to cool, picking up a jade paper-knife and plucking with it at the blotter. Vera Gorringe's voice came quickly across the room.

"You've found more support, have you, for this idea?"

He glanced up.

"It doesn't win you yet?"

"Certainly not. But it's begun to persuade me, just a little."

He nodded, looking down and digging another flake of the white blotting-paper with the point of the smooth green blade.

"Yes, I've found more support. Some from Mrs. Martin this morning; some from Freddie, at lunch. He's been to see the Medical Superintendent at Broadmoor. One or two interesting points came up. He didn't feel they were particularly interesting; but I do. One: Speight tried to escape about a month after he was sent there."

"I should imagine a lot of them do."

"That's what Freddie said, yes. I think it's right, too. But let's suppose that Speight was telling the absolute truth in court. He might, then, have regained complete memory after a month at the asylum—and tried to escape and clear himself by finding the assailant: the murderer."

"Why didn't he merely see the authorities and describe the man he'd remembered? And give his portrait to them as well?"

"He wouldn't trust authority. Authority had sent him to an asylum, and he was sane. Bitterness alone would have impelled him to escape and clear himself by finding the man who'd killed Joanna. He would have turned to authority only when he'd got irrefutable evidence. Just as he'll turn to them now, if he succeeds."

"This is still supposition."

"It is."

"Even in your own mind?"

"Yes."

Miss Gorringe nodded.

"All right, I admit that the attempted escape could be explained like that. Could. There's more?"

"Two: Speight kept news-clippings of the trial. He hid them for a year. It's believed that before they were found he must have read them almost every day."

"What does Frisnay say?"

"You tell me."

She said: "Paranoia. He kept the clippings to gloat over."

"Yes, that's Frisnay's explanation. Perhaps it's too obvious and too simple. Suppose Speight had lost his memory as well as consciousness, at the scene of the killing: news-clippings would have helped him to a great extent. They would even have helped him find his man—among the reports and the publicity."

Miss Gorringe left her desk and began wandering absently across the room, stopping to peer at ornaments, to brush the ash off the Siamese's head, to adjust a crooked picture.

"That's good, Hugo. Not superlative, but good. Anything else?"

"Three: Speight has made many drawings of this face. Some he hasn't tried to conceal—perhaps they didn't come off—but others he secreted. I'm ready to believe that he might have had to make a hundred such drawings before he was satisfied. Satisfied that he'd made as nearly perfect a portrait of the assailant as his memory allowed, and as his art enabled him."

"But it didn't take him two years—"

Bishop looked up from the blotter.

"It's doubtful. But it might easily have taken him two years—to escape."

Miss Gorringe turned from a Japanese print and looked at him with her colorless eyes.

"All right, Hugo. That could fit, too. I admit

that some of this is building up well. In theory.
Is there more?"

"Four: I've told you already that Thelma, Tasman has her own theory about Speight's escape.
She thinks—if she wasn't lying to me, and that's
quite possible—that she mentioned Tasman's
name once too often, during her interviews with
Speight at Broadmoor."

Miss Gorringe came slowly towards his desk,
and at last stood patiently, her arms folded, her
eyes regarding him steadily across the bric-á-
brac as he went on, gazing at her in return.

"Speight believes—according to our supposition—that somewhere in London, or England
at least, there's a man who murdered Joanna
Martin. That man is the Person—we'll give him
a capital P—whom we and Speight are looking
for. Wouldn't it be natural, or at the least con-
ceivable, for the Person to make it his business
to keep Thelma Speight's company as closely as
possible? So that he would know immediately
if Speight showed any sign of a real attempt to
clear himself?"

He sat back in his chair, keeping his eyes on
Vera Gorringe, trying, even as he went on, to
glimpse a reaction in her own.

"Speight said in court that there was another
man on the bombed-site. That there was a murderer, free in London, unknown, unnamed. Our
Person. Speight would realize that the Person
appreciated his own danger. That danger could

come only from Speight. From Broadmoor. From the one mind that knew of the Person's existence."

Miss Gorringe did not move. Her eyes expressed nothing. Bishop finished deliberately:

"The Person must then try to be in contact with his enemy as closely as possible—on a mental plane. So that he would be warned if the danger took shape. The best medium would be Thelma, the enemy's wife and constant visitor."

He dropped the paper-knife to the desk.

He said: "Speight believes that our Person *is* Victor Tasman. Do you?"

16th

MOVE

♛HE WAS a small, thin man, bald as a ball. His nose was hooked, as if years of sniffing at articles brought to him for sale had made it occupationally malformed. His shoulders were slightly humped, their blades visible in outline beneath the jacket he wore, so that he seemed like a bird of prey that was constantly just about to open its pinions—but had never had to trouble, with so long and so certain a beak.

He leaned forward, also after the manner of the vulture; but this was simply because the light in this littered place was always so dim that the eyes must be held close to their subject.

There seemed to be no actual counter in his

little shop; but there was an oblong mound of china ornaments, glassware, fishing tackle, cameras, cast-off clothing, chemistry sets, attaché-cases, stamp collections, binoculars, chess sets, horse brasses and golf clubs that might conceal such a counter beneath its polyglot confusion.

Along the three walls of the shop there seemed to be no actual shelves, yet there must obviously have been some system of support for the kit-bags, rucksacks, mackintoshes, dressing-gowns, gas capes, thigh boots, gym shoes, tennis balls, marble clocks, bowler hats, fencing masks, violet-ray kits, ping-pong bats, tins, basins and boxes.

In the fourth wall there was set a long shop window, suggested by a half-dozen chinks of daylight among the heap of crockery, tennis rackets, air-guns, mouth organs, bronze ornaments, egg-timers, carpet-beaters, alarm-clocks, stuffed parrots, white collars, fly-swats, colanders, Japanese scimitars and teapot stands.

It was through these half-dozen chinks that the thin bald man peered at the faces of people looking through his windowpane at all those things that were there. Many a potential customer's character was analyzed by facial assessment through these chinks, while he stood assessing the value or otherwise of the article that had caught his eye.

The thin man ran his shop on a reasonable assumption: now that he had assembled his stock in such variety and profusion, there could be nothing here that *someone* did not want. The only factor that denied him a stupendous trade was that each particular *someone* was hard put to it to find the thing he wanted, among so many that he certainly did not.

The shopkeeper had already studied the face of the woman who now entered his shop. Through the largest of the chinks he had seen her stop to look at something in the window; and he had amused himself as usual by trying to judge what article it was that had caught her attention.

He felt he had failed. Unless it was the costume brooch.

He bowed over his hands to the lady.

She was in her late twenties, beautifully groomed, simply dressed, good-looking. A model, perhaps.

Even before she spoke, he knew that she did not want the costume brooch. This lady was not at ease. Through the chink and through the glass of the window he had glimpsed her face; he had not discerned the expression of her mouth, her eyes.

Gravely she had come in here for something less trivial than a brooch. Passing the window, she had seen by pure chance an article that she must, at this moment, value. So much so that she had made up her mind to acquire. But not without an effort.

"There's—something in your window . . . "

He smiled.

"Many things, madam," he said.

She did not smile. She said:

"The little black gun."

He raised his brows. They lifted like thick feathers against the parchment skin. He had almost forgotten the little black gun was there.

He said softly: "I will get it for you."

She waited, not yet regretting her impulse. The gun had been lying among the confusion in the window; for an instant her mind had not registered it as significant, and she had nearly walked on. Then the links became suddenly joined: the series of mental values and conditions that formed a sum-total with the quickness of thought.

She had entered the shop. The gun must be bought.

With the cunning and the delicacy of a fly-fisherman's sudden cast, the man picked the gun from the window, and left the hundred other objects undisturbed.

He turned and held it on his palm for the lady to see. She made no move to take it, to examine it. She said quietly:

"Does it work?"

He weighed it in his hand, smiling.

"I have never seen it work, madam; but I bought it from a person who would not have possessed such a thing had it not worked perfectly. And see, it is well oiled. The mechanism"—he directed the short black barrel away from the lady—"is in excellent trim."

He squeezed the trigger six times in swift succession. The spring was good. He opened the shell—chamber for her inspection.

"And see, the condition is as new."

The lady nodded.

"Have you suitable ammunition?"

He sucked his breath in, closing the chamber and moving spider-like round the mound that concealed his counter, his thin hand weighing the gun. He glanced at her, his small head cocked like a bird's.

"I may have, madam. I may have, yes. But have you a license?"

She looked downwards at her handbag, then up again.

"Well, no. I imagine I must have the gun before I can get a license."

He considered the price of the gun. It had gone up three pounds in the last five seconds.

He said: "It is not always easy to get a gun license. One must have reasons for carrying a fire-arm. They always ask, you see."

He looked at her.

She opened her bag.

"I shall be able to satisfy them. How much is the gun?"

He weighed it again. The lady was impatient with this talk of licenses. It was the gun she must have. Its price rose another two pounds.

"With the few clips of ammunition that I think I could find, madam, the gun would be twelve pounds."

She closed her bag. Her voice was taut.

"I haven't that amount with me."

He gave a slight bow over the gun.

"I would accept your cheque, madam."

"I'd prefer to pay cash. I have about ten pounds here."

He was sad. He looked at his beautiful little gun, and then at the beautiful little lady. He admitted in his mind that it was the perfect weapon for that small pale hand. He could not, of course, judge whether that particular bullet among the few clips that he would sell the lady would be the perfect visitor for her lover's heart ... or her husband's ... or whoever's heart it was that beat to her disadvantage.

He was a salesman, not Solomon.

He said: "Ten pounds," and considered such a low price. The lady said nothing. He looked up. "Would it be possible for you to bring in the other two pounds later?"

She said: "I shan't be this way again."

He smiled, charmingly.

"Then I won't neglect my chance of doing you a service, madam." He put the gun tenderly on to the heap of rollerskates and went to burrow among various gaps and crannies for the ammunition. "It will keep you a few moments longer in my shop," his voice murmured among the banjos and the violins, "and my shop is so dusty and dark. Few ladies as beautiful as you come in here, madam. You bring it life."

He found the clips of ammunition, and tossed one in his hand, turning with a gentle smile. He added: "And take away death."

She neither moved nor spoke. She looked at the ammunition clips for a moment longer, then looked away, opening her bag again and taking out money.

Wiping the surplus oil from the gun, the thin man said: "Shall I demonstrate how the clips are to be fitted, madam, or are you familiar—"

"No. No, thank you, it isn't necessary."

He bowed over the gun as he wrapped it with the clips. The lady paid.

She put the parcel into her bag, and went from the dark, dusty shop.

"Good day to you, madam."

"Thank you, good-bye."

Her shoes clicked over-loudly on the pavement, hurrying from the doorway. Her handbag felt unexpectedly heavy.

Hugo Bishop stopped, with a cheerful smile.

"Well, hello," he said.

17th

MOVE

SHE COULD not, for the moment, return the cheerful smile or the friendly greeting. The recent memory of the darkened cubicle, the memory, too, of a moment ago when the man had said *take away death*, the awareness of the weight in her handbag, and now the sudden shock of the meeting were all too much to contend with, until she had time to relax.

"Did you follow me here, Mr. Bishop?"

He wrinkled his brow, slightly amused.

"Well, no. Did you follow me?"

She drew a breath, looking away from him at the traffic, at the people along the pavements, at all the ordinary scenic life from which she now felt almost cut off. Almost she was a stranger to the world she had known and grown up with; a woman apart from ordinary sane people, with a gun in her bag and a lie on her tongue and the fear of the mad in her heart.

She said quickly:

"I'm sorry. That was an odd thing to think."

She looked at her watch.

"Quite understandable," said Bishop easily. "Or as understandable as most coincidences are. I'm waiting for them to finish checking the oil—just across the road there; and you're doing some shopping."

She forced a smile.

"That's reasonable," she said.

He turned with her along the pavement.

"The only unreasonable thing," he murmured, "is that my garage and your shop happen to be opposite. In fact, I was putting in time by staring with fascination into that extraordinary window. It must contain everything in the world."

She glanced at him. He looked ahead.

He said: "Except braces. I couldn't see any braces. I don't need any, but you know what I mean—one somehow *expects* a pair of braces among the Japanese scimitars and the egg-timers."

After a second or two she said: "I'm afraid I must hurry. There's the last show to cover."

He stopped, digging his hands into his pockets and smiling down at her.

"Let me run you there. They'll have finished the car by now."

"It—actually isn't far."

"Then you'll be early."

She turned with him, crossing the road. The 1920 Rolls-Royce stood at the curbside outside the garage. A small child was regarding it, swinging a catapult nonchalantly by its elastic.

"What 'appened to the man with the red flag, mister?" he asked with over-bright innocence.

Bishop got in.

"I ran him over," he said. "He looked rather like you."

Thelma closed her door, straightening her skirt. Bishop asked: "Which way do we go?"

"Is Grosvenor Street on your route?"

"It is now."

He started the engine. They were driving along Piccadilly before she said simply:

"Why were you talking about Joanna Martin?"

"This morning?"

She nodded. "Yes."

He shrugged.

"Most people are. Her ghost is in the news."

He watched her profile for an instant. Her expression was calm; it had the intense calm of deliberate and inflexible control. Her hands rested on the bag; her neat white shoes were together.

"But why," she asked steadily, "did you talk about her so suddenly, at the du Vancet show?

And without any preamble?"

He drove past Bond Street, where he should
have turned up. He said:

"What time have you to be in Grosvenor Street?"

"At six."

He looked down at the dashboard.

"Twenty minutes," he said. "Let's drive through
the park."

Her head turned; she looked at him for a moment. Then: "All right."

The car rounded Wellington Memorial and
slid between the great stone pillars, turning left.
The six-cylinder engine made so little sound that
there was the intimacy of almost total silence
inside the saloon, save for the passing of other
cars.

He held his cigarette case in front of her. She
took one, lighting it.

"You're not smoking?" she said.

"Not just now."

Nearing Albert Gate, he slowed.

"Mind if we stop for a while?"

"No, I don't mind."

The whisper of the tires died away; the ignition
switch clicked quietly; the needle on the instrument dials moved to zero, save for the tempera-
tures. The smoke from her cigarette was drawn
to the open window and swirled free.

He said quietly: "I had my reasons for throwing
the subject of Joanna Martin into the conversation. I'm sorry it had to be done so brusquely.

There wasn't time for an introduction to the dead."

"Please don't make it sound so horrible."

"Forgive me."

She hesitated, gripping the handbag. Then she said it aloud: "Today you've seemed different from last night. A different person. Last night you came when I needed someone to talk to just to be with. Another human, who'd protect me if anything happened."

"Last night when I came I found you terrified. Anyone would have helped you, then."

She shook her head and her dark hair moved softly. "They wouldn't—not quite as you did." She turned to face him fully, watching his eyes. "There was something about you—a quality of quiet strength—I can't really define it."

He smiled. He said: "I'm the original strong, silent man."

"Yes, I think you would be, if you didn't try to be so facetious."

He watched her eyes, as she watched his. He thought hers were quite lovely; the loneliness in them now made them more than merely beautiful: it appealed to his male instinct to protect women, and it touched his vanity as a man. He didn't have any illusions about these things. He said:

"I don't try to be facetious. It's an unfortunate accident, possibly of birth. Or possibly I was trying not to make things sound so horrible, as you asked."

She looked away, through the windscreen to where there were two bay horses being walked down from the Serpentine road. Faintly she could hear their hooves.

"Has anything happened," she murmured, "to make you different and rather hostile?"

He leaned his forearms on the wheel, looking with her through the screen.

"Suppose we talk seriously for a few minutes. Who are you trying to shield?"

Her small head turned again, was moved by the question.

"I don't understand you."

"Are you trying to shield Victor Tasman, or Maurice Jerrold, or Rex Willison, or someone whose name I don't know—someone called The Gent—"

"I don't *understand*—"

"I hope you don't, but I'm not sure—"

"Shield them from what?"

"Hanging."

She caught her breath. When he turned his head slowly he found her staring at him. Her lips were parted, and now softly she whispered: "Hanging?"

He said: "Yes."

She spoke quickly and urgently.

"Please go on talking—I know I must understand this somehow. But, coming on top of everything else, I can't seem to—take it in."

Her hand was on his arm; the fingers tightened.

"Please go on talking, Hugo."

He said: "You're brilliant."

"How brilliant?"

"Or sincere. What I'm saying is easy to explain. The police are working on a theory, in their search for Mervyn Speight—"

"Then you are from the police—"

"No, but I happen to know something of what goes on at the Yard. Their theory is that Mervyn has an obsession. It might be truth or untruth that he believes in; but whichever it is, it's thought possible that he's managed to contact you—and managed to convince you that he's right."

Her head moved in bewilderment. "But you know he hasn't contacted me. You know the thought of speaking to him terrifies me."

"Yes, I know your obsession, too."

Her small hand left his arm and a shiver passed through her body. She closed her eyes, leaning her head against the door pillar. Her voice was dry and toneless.

"I don't know what to believe in, or who to trust. I don't know who you are, or what you're trying to make me say, or make me do. All I know is that I'm afraid of Mervyn, afraid of the mad."

Gently he said: "Yes, most people are afraid of the mad. You must be even more afraid, because as a young wife you saw your husband tried for murder and committed to an asylum. You have this fear as an obsession and it's riding you now."

Her eyes did not open. She said nothing. He touched her hand; it was cold. He went on quietly, the words rising and falling in the silence of the car.

"Thelma, the theory is that Mervyn believes that he's innocent. That someone else killed the Martin girl—as he swore at his trial. That he's broken out to find this person and either to kill him out of hand for what he did to Mervyn, or to force him to confess to the murder. There are several pointers to this theory; there are even pointers to Mervyn's belief being true."

Slowly her eyes opened, and the light from the windscreen lay lambently on the blue of them between the narrowed lids. They were scarcely wide enough to reveal expression as she watched his face.

"There are some things I can't tell you," he said softly. "But there are other theories, some of them logical, others intuitive or even imaginative. One is that you've known, yourself, the real killer of Joanna Martin, since her death and Mervyn's trial. And that you're trying to protect him because he means more to you than Mervyn does—"

"You think that?" she whispered.

"No. It's one of the many theories that have come up from long discussions and conjecture. I want you to know about it because I want you to know that the search for Mervyn is only the central theme of a whole web of suspicion;

and that you are more deeply involved than you think."

He pressed her hand. "I want you to know where you stand."

She said almost wearily: "Go on, Hugo."

"The theory about you isn't being seriously considered or followed up. Another one is: that Mervyn himself believes in it, and is trying to prove it true."

"He thinks I let him be convicted, and sent to Broadmoor, when I could have prevented it?"

"Worse—that you're living with the man who killed Joanna Martin. Or at least know him, and keep his secret."

A strange half-smile came to her mouth.

"Poor mad Mervyn. Before the marriage was a year old, we'd stopped loving each other. But I didn't think this could occur to him."

"He was sent to Broadmoor, Thelma. It's very probable that justice was done, and that he's insane. You must remember that these theories are no more than theories, so far. Until I told you about them, you believed—and maybe still believe—that Mervyn escaped because of jealousy."

"Because of Victor."

"Yes."

"Do you still believe that, more than the other things?"

"I've begun to doubt it."

After a little while she said:

"How can I help in all this?"

"I'd like you to tell me two things."

"If I can."

"Do you believe Mervyn killed that girl?"

She leaned her head away from the door-pillar. Her eyes opened fully and remained on his.

"If I doubt it now, it's for the first time."

Her hand moved to drop the cigarette end into the ashtray on the panel. He offered her another, and struck a match for her. As the little flame leapt he asked her:

"The second thing is, did Victor tell you he was going to Bristol—before yesterday morning?"

She considered for a moment.

"I'm not sure. I can't remember."

"When do you first remember hearing that he was going?"

"I think on Friday morning."

"Yesterday morning."

She nodded. "Yes."

"But it's possible that he mentioned it at some time before that—say, on Thursday."

"He might have. I don't remember. So many things have happened—"

"Yes, of course."

"Why is it important, Hugo?"

"It might not be. I believe you when you say that you thought Mervyn guilty—even if now you might find a doubt here and there after what I've said. But it isn't impossible—except for you—to theorize that Victor didn't believe Mervyn guilty: didn't believe it for the strongest reason possible—because he himself was guilty, and made it his business after the trial to keep as close to you as he could, by any means he could find—"

"Hugo, it's—"

"Absurd, yes, I know it's absurd. I don't expect you to think otherwise." He paused. Then: "I believe you love him."

"I do. But that doesn't distort my judgment."

"I don't think Victor knows anything about the killing. You've told me that he doesn't even know why you can't marry him—because you're Mervyn's wife. I believe that. I'll go on believing it until something comes up that makes me doubt it—"

"You think something will?"

"The impossible is only the thing that happens when you never expected it."

She straightened in her seat and spoke slowly to him.

"Now I know why you seem a different person today. You're wallowing in theories and you can't think straight. You don't even know if you ought to help me or put the police on to me—"

He said: "I at least know that. A lot of these theories have been broken down while we've talked. That's why I wanted to see you. When I met you outside the junk-shop I didn't know if you were involved in this murder or not. I didn't know if Tasman was, although one strong factor made me doubt it. Now I've heard you talk and I know that you and he are clear. Not because of your tacit assurance alone, but because of the whole drift of your reaction—"

"What strong factor made you doubt that Victor was involved?"

He considered for a moment, but there seemed no reason why he should keep it back now.

"When I met Mervyn last night, he showed me a portrait of a man. Everything seems to point to that man as the murderer, if it isn't Mervyn. I've seen the man in the portrait today. It wasn't Victor Tasman."

"Who was it?"

He took his arms from the steering wheel, and switched on the ignition.

"Mervyn has broken out of Broadmoor to find this man. He's either Joanna Martin's killer or a mere obsession of an insane mind."

He started the engine and dropped the lever into gear. He said:

"Can you think who it might be? Who would Mervyn suspect?"

She stared ahead through the screen. Her voice was dull.

"Apart from Victor?" she said.

"Yes, other than Victor."

She smoked her cigarette, drawing on it deeply. The smoke eddied inside the car before it was tugged gently away by the slipstream.

"I don't know," she said tonelessly. "My mind is normal. Mervyn's is mad. I can't guess what obsessions come to the insane. I don't know."

The Rolls-Royce turned right and glided between the balustrades over the Serpentine.

Bishop said quietly:

"Well, if it occurs to you, let me know. It's rather important."

She said nothing until the car swung into Park Lane. She turned her head to look at him, as if suddenly reaching a decision.

"Hugo, I don't quite know where I stand with you, but I don't think you're against me."

"That's perfectly right."

"I just want to know—how much I can count on you. If anything happens."

"You mean dangerous to yourself?"

She nodded. The car moved silent into Grosvenor Street.

"I expect I mean that," she said.

"You can count on me all the way. That's never changed."

She said nothing for a moment. Then: "I just wanted to know, Hugo." She put out her cigarette. "I'm going into Park Court—anywhere here will do."

He slowed.

"Are you booked up after this show?"

"Yes. The trade and my people are going on to the Lotus Bowl. I'm afraid I've got to be there."

"Cocktails?"

"Yes."

He stopped the car. He said:

"Are the gates crashable?"

She smiled faintly.

"Why?"

"I'd like you to meet someone."

"Must it be at the party?"

"It'd be more interesting."

Her smile went from her mouth.

"Is it important, Hugo?"

"Yes, it is, a bit."

"All right. Tell them you're Press, and if there's any trouble, ask for me."

She got out of the car, standing for a moment with her small gloved hand on the window ledge.

"I'm glad you'll be coming. Who is it I'm to meet?"

"Lady Verisham, a dear old thing I picked up at a garden fête. But you'll find her interesting."

"I hope it's mutual."

She took her hand from the window ledge. He moved the gears into first. He said:

"I should warn you she's a bit nervous. Don't let anything go off in your handbag."

The engine gave a rising murmur of acceleration. He turned into New Bond Street and headed south. It was just six o'clock and he had fixed things dead on schedule.

18th

MOVE

♛ THE DIAL span back.
The ringing tone ran for five seconds; then there was a click as the connection opened.

"Lotus Bowl."

"Good evening. You have a cocktail-party, I believe, following the fashion show at Park Court."

"We have, yes."

"I'd like to ask what time it starts."

"Seven o'clock, sir. But it depends on how long the show overruns."

"I understand. Many thanks."

He hung up.

From her desk Miss Gorringe said:

"What do you want me to wear, Hugo?"

"Your mink tiara, dear."

Patiently she said: "Who am I supposed to be?"

He looked steadily at the cover of *Autosport*, which bore the photograph of the new XK-120 at Le Mans, mounted by the fabulous Moss.

He said absently: "What?"

Patiently she said: "Who am I supposed to be? I will repeat that at ten-second intervals for those who are still coming in."

"Lady Verisham, a dear old baggage I picked up at a horse fair."

"The name is reasonable. I dislike the description."

"I thought perhaps you might. Let's say, then, a little bit of fluff I picked up at a carpet sale."

Patiently she said: "I take it I'm supposed to be an English lady of some fifty summers and with an interest in fashions."

"That's that birdie. Lorgnettes, jet lockets, dodo-feather fan and tweed galoshes."

Miss Gorringe restrained a sigh. She asked mildly:

"How long have I to change?"

He checked his watch.

"Thirty minutes."

"Streuth," said Lady Verisham, and hurried out of the room. Bishop went on admiring the XK-120 until the telephone rang. He picked it up.

"Yes?"

"Freddie here, Hugo."

"Dear boy."

Frisnay overlooked this and said:

"I've been doing a lot of thinking since lunch."

"And how are you now?"

"What d'you make of the Tasman woman in the light of her new role?"

Bishop said: "You mean now that she's toting a rod?"

"Yes."

"So your man was shopping with her, was he?"

"Of course. He had more trouble keeping out of your way than out of hers."

"He shouldn't be so sensitive. I'd only have given him a friendly shout across the road. Why do *you* think she's bought the thing, Freddie?"

"To shoot someone with."

"I admit I didn't imagine she got it to disinfect the candelabra."

"So you've no ideas?"

"I may have, but they're not necessarily in the public domain. Is there anything else I might be reluctant to answer for you?"

Frisnay uttered a grunt. He added:

"At lunch you said you'd been to see Joanna Martin's sister-in-law. With what idea?"

"With no idea. I never went to see her."

There was a silent pause.

"I didn't mishear you," Freddie complained.

"I'm glad. Because I didn't say that. I said I'd been chatting with her. I actually went to see Joanna's mother."

"Why her mother?"

"Well, I mean, why not? She's probably the comfortable kind of body who'd have given me a cup of tea. Whereas I was obliged to render the sis-in-law a fraction sloshed on mother's ruin before she'd regain consciousness."

"What did you learn?" Frisnay asked.

"All about Joanna's young gentlemen. Apparently she carried on something shocking with the boys o' the village. In point of fact, I don't think she was any better than she should be, if you comprehend old English."

Frisnay said: "We know all about Martin."

"Ah. Then you don't want me to tell you what I heard."

"I'm not suggesting that."

"Frankly, Freddie, I didn't learn all that much, but it got a few ideas creeping round inside my withered scalp, and, what with one thing and another, I think I've added two and two together. The one thing that bothers me is that the answer appears to be five."

Frisnay said patiently:

"Just go on talking. You might reveal something interesting if only by accident."

"I'll save our time. Have you any records at the Yard about a man called The Gent?"

"Several. It's not uncommon. Any hoodlum who sports a Woolworth's tie-pin gets the name."

"Well, check on the lot. The one I'm talking

about was described as a toff—business-man sort—had a car—wasn't young—he was big. Unquote."

Frisnay said:

"That narrows it. Last heard of in London about two years ago?"

"According to sis-in-law."

"All right, we'll check. Was he involved with Joanna Martin?"

"You could put it like that. You could also check on these: Emmerson—had a car and some money—little man with glasses—Joanna tried to get too much from him. Next, Sidney—a flash type—smoked cigars—cocky little rat—wore rings. He also attempted to interest sis-in-law in proposals worse than death, but she said the gipsies had warned her. That's the lot, Freddie."

Frisnay did not answer for a few seconds. Apparently he had been making notes. Now he said:

"This could be interesting, however vague the descriptions. Why did you hold out on me about these people, at lunch?"

Bishop slowly closed one eye at Chu Yi-Hsin, who was dozing on her haunches at the end of his desk. He said gently:

"At that time, Frederick, you weren't inclined to consider looking for anyone except Speight."

There was a pause. Then:

"Ideas change."

"It must have been the li-chee."

Frisnay said quietly: "Everything I've said over this phone—and everything I've even implied—is absolutely unofficial, Hugo."

"You know you shouldn't talk without your lawyer present, I'm a dangerous man."

Frisnay didn't reply. Bishop added:

"But I've also tried to give you some leads. If they get you anywhere, I hope you'll let me know."

"I'll let you know."

"Thanks. I shall be here until about seven. From about seven to about eight I'll be at the Lotus Bowl drinking cocktails on Film Fabrics Limited—I'm gate-crashing, so don't let them say I'm not there—then after that I'll be dining Gorry at West's until about ten, I should think."

"I'll try to reach you if there's a real development."

"I wish you would. Something cosy isn't unlikely to develop at my end, by the way. Where can I find you if necessary?"

Frisnay said: "I'm here until midnight. If I'm not in, they'll get me on the radio—I'll be out with the heavy mob. All right?"

"All right, Freddie."

They parted. Bishop stared for a few minutes at the telephone dial, and then got up after making a note on his blotter.

Changing into a dinner-jacket in his room, he thought about Thelma buying the gun. That was a queer thing to have done. He had driven her through Hyde Park and talked to her partly to find out why she had done that. He still couldn't see a reason.

To defend herself if Speight showed up?

He doubted it, but her obsession might be that serious. She might have bought the thing on an impulse. He had not seen her approaching the shop—his car had turned the corner a minute later than would have been ideal. He had just seen her going into the doorway. Had she been passing the window when she'd seen the gun, and decided to buy it? Or had she seen it there before, and decided to buy it at this particular time?

All he had seen was the gun being taken from the window, No other customers had been in the shop at that time.

He adjusted his bow-tie.

Thelma, honey, why the gun?

He slipped into the dinner-jacket, checked the pockets and filled the cigarette case. His watch was at five minutes to seven.

As he was leaving the room the extension phone rang and he picked it up.

"Yes?"

He put a cigarette between his lips, feeling for the lighter.

"Is that Hugo Bishop?"

"That's right."

He lit the cigarette.

"This is Mervyn Speight."

He dropped the lighter into his pocket, took the cigarette from his mouth and said:

"Good evening."

19th

MOVE

♛ MISS GORRINGE came into the room with something of an air. She had chosen—in her hurried thirty minutes—one of the few of her evening gowns that Bishop had not seen before. It was black; it was simple; it was—since it had been designed and cut by masters—superb.

Her blued, piled coiffure, set this morning by a coiffeur who was also a master, gave her three inches and a perfect halo.

Her entrance, at this moment, was studied and faultless. It was a shame, because Hugo did not even glance up.

She said in her most gracious tone:

"The old baggage from the horse fair has arrived."

Bishop added two more names to the list on his blotter, put down the pencil and looked up. He allowed the pause of admiration that was necessary to the compliment.

"Magnificent," he smiled.

She curtsied, with an over-styled flourish.

"A little late, Hugo, but still acceptable. Thank you."

His cigarette was half-burned. He doused it in the ash-bowl. He said charmingly:

"In any other circumstances, Lady Verisham, nothing would have delighted me more than to escort so captivating a companion to the Lotus Bowl."

She frowned slightly.

"Other circumstances? Aren't we going, you brute?"

"Later, perhaps, but not at once. Circumstances have changed in the last five minutes."

"So have I practically. Apparently for nothing. What's happened?"

He came into the middle of the room, still admiring her *ensemble*. Then he said:

"Speight's just telephoned. He wants to meet me."

She dropped her evening bag on to the davenport and sat down slowly.

"Oh. Technical hitch. You're going to meet him?"

"Yes, I think so."

"Now?"

"Now or never. He was very edgy."

"Tell me more."

"Oh, we didn't talk long. Seems he's being pretty well run to earth by the police search. Freddie's mob are just everywhere and he's been seen twice and almost got taken."

Vera Gorringe took her cigarette holder, fitted a du Maurier and let him light it for her.

"Where is the trysting-place, Hugo?"

"Oh," he said, "just around."

"Cagey."

He shrugged slightly.

"Reasons." He was frowning in thought.

She said: "You seem worried. Is it going to be dangerous, meeting Speight?"

"M'm? No, I shouldn't think so. Unless he's crazy."

"It's an opinion Broadmoor might support. I don't think you ought to go without telling me where to look for your body."

She was almost serious. When a case was at its hottest, Hugo Bishop often forgot to be cautious in his excitement. It was at these moments that Vera Gorringe wished he were a philatelist or an interior decorator, or something reasonable like that.

At these moments she would often have left his employ, except that—paradoxically—it was these moments that made her job too fascinating to leave.

Bishop said vaguely: "If my body has to be looked for, the police are going to find it p.b.q., because Speight's the only danger, and they're all round him now. So don't worry your pretty blue-rinse about that."

"I'm relieved to hear it, Hugo. The fact that your cadaver's going to be easy to locate is a great consolation. I suppose there's no chance of your survival?"

He stood looking down at her. She really made a study in *Vogue*. He was sorry he wasn't taking her to the Lotus Bowl immediately.

"Unless you've anything better to do," he said, "it might be interesting to stay near the telephone. I shall be with Speight in ten minutes. I doubt if the discussion's going to take long. Suppose I ring you in, say, half an hour?"

She got up from the davenport.

"All right, Hugo."

He looked nice in his dinner-jacket. Slim and quite tall, he had good grey eyes and could look at people very straight. And he had a kind mind. If Vera Gorringe ever adopted a favorite nephew, she'd apply for this person.

He went to the door, opening it.

Miss Gorringe called:

"I'll stay by the telephone unless I get bored."

"In case you get bored, you might try to find out where those people are at the moment. Their names are on the blotter."

She moved to his enormous desk and looked at the latest scribblings.

She said: "Do you want them to come here?"

"No, I just want to know where to find them, later tonight."

"I'll do my best."

"There's a good girl."

As he went out she called:

"Take care of yourself, you young idiot."

The door closed.

Miss Gorringe sat down at her employer's desk, checked the directory for the first name on his blotter, and picked up the receiver of the telephone. Her hand was shaking very slightly, but she ignored it. He'd be back.

Clouds were in from the west, and lay half across London. In Caledonian Road there were still a few faint sunbeams; in Kensington it was almost twilight, and shadows were deepening.

The Thames came running softly, apace with the cloudbank; below Westminster Bridge the water was already dark. A string of long-boats threaded beneath the span of it, down to the gunwales with timber. Towards Blackfriars a police launch was nosing a creamy wake along the southern bank.

On the Embankment, between Vauxhal Bridge Road and Chelsea Bridge, Speight crouched

watching the water. Behind him was the parados
of a wharf, and it protected him. If they came
from the land to look in this place, he would hear
them first. If they came by water, he would see
them first.

He waited, chilled, cramped, nursing his bitterness, his stomach an empty shell and his eyes
dull with waiting. The sweete Thaymes ran softly
by.

From Big Ben came the chime of the quarter. The fringe, of the long-boats' wake reached
the wharf-side, touching the timber and leaping
back, wave upon wave. From Battersea power
station a thick swell of smoke was drawing out
along the horizon, seemingly motionless save at
the source.

Speight crouched, stubble-faced and with an
aching back. It was fifteen minutes since he had
made his way here from the telephone box; already his limbs were stiff again with nervous
tension.

He listened for sounds—the dangerous sound
of a footstep, a voice, an oar, the drag of slowing
tires behind the wharf, the distant passage of the
hunt.

Twice they had seen him today; once he had
gone running like a stag, his feet sliding on the
dusty tarmac of an alleyway, his hands flying out
against a wall, the flesh of one palm stripped on
the hard face of the bricks, his ears agonized

by the tramp of feet, the shrilling whistle, the opening of doors.

His heart was all that had been in his mouth today; his stomach was like a husk. His head lolled on him, lulled with the fatal charm of creeping sleep that had not been to him since thirty hours ago. Sleep was as soft, and as sweet, and as beautiful as Delilah; and now, for him, as treacherous.

He jerked the dream away, the dream of the slow, dark water that his dull eyes watched, the sound of its lullaby. He could feel the red of his eyes' rims, feel it burn in his brain. He must sit up straight, drag himself to the high mountain-top of the crate that was his seat.

Bishop called softly: "Speight."

His breath snatched in his throat and his head moved as if from a blow. In the shadows of the wharf he could make out the white sheen of a shirt-front against the darker clothes. His voice was a dry grunt.

"Bishop?"

If it were someone else, it scarcely seemed to matter now. At Broadmoor, there was sleep.

Softly: "Yes. Don't get up."

From the depths of Speight's bruised mind there came a queer little quirk of humor. He murmured:

"This time it's me caught napping."

Bishop moved towards him, turning his back

to the river—the one direction from which he could be seen. The white of his shirt would extend visibility by a hundred yards in this light. Speight sat hunched, looking up at him, his eyes vein-laced, his face dark with stubble, his hair tangled. He hadn't had to overdo his appearance to look like just another tramp along the waterfront. It had come naturally, out of hunger, and sleeplessness, and flight.

Bishop dropped a packet onto his knees.

"Sandwiches," he said softly. "Ham." He crouched down, protecting the white paper from observation across the river. "Are you cold?"

For minutes there was no answer. Speight broke small crumbs from the bread, slowly and painstakingly. His stomach urged him to crush the whole sandwich into his mouth and force it down. He knew that, if he did, the agony would cost him his consciousness, after so many hours of hunger.

Soon he said:

"I didn't expect you."

"But I said I was coming."

"I didn't think you meant it."

"Why shouldn't I?"

Speight shook his head, and for a moment his palate was a flow of delight as it found the salt taste of the ham in the bread.

Bishop waited for a few minutes, then:

"You wanted to talk to me. We haven't long. The police are everywhere, and soon they'll be down here. There's a routine check going on—a five-mile dragnet across London."

Looking at the man, hearing the jaded voice, he remembered Gorry's anxiety. Speight could not have kicked a dog away, as he was now.

Speight said:

"Last time we met, you offered to help me."

"It still holds. In fact, I've been helping you quite a bit since then. Unless it was you who murdered Joanna."

Speight's head turned.

He said: "Unless?"

"Yes. I mean contrary to popular belief."

"Your belief isn't popular?"

Bishop said: "Not at the moment. But you can tell me I'm wrong."

After a while Speight looked away from him, to the river. "You must be the only one. Except the one who did it."

Bishop looked along the water-front. It seemed deserted. Crates were stacked against the walls of the wharf; cranes stuck out their ugly metallic necks, peering for prey to hang; the roofs made an obtuse-angled pattern against the cloud-fields. Nothing moved. He turned back to Speight.

"We can't stay here long. Before we go—"

"Before *we* go?"

"I want you to come with me, if we can get through the hunt. Will you come?"

Speight broke a larger piece from a sandwich, putting it into his mouth.

"If I stay here," he said, "I'll get taken. I might as well come with you."

"There are a few better reasons, but we'll leave them for the moment. Before we go, I want to know a few things. Did you kill the girl?"

Speight ate half the sandwich. This bread was more important than questions, than freedom, than murder. Soon he answered:

"At my trial I got tired of saying no. Sometimes, at the asylum, I told people yes, just to feel what it was like to agree with fifty million other people. It never seemed to matter much which I said. You really want to know?"

"I do."

Speight said: "No, I didn't kill the girl."

"You believe you saw the man who did?"

"I saw him."

"Was that his portrait you showed me last night?"

"Yes. It was his portrait."

"Will you show it to me again?"

"Now?"

"Yes, now."

He took out the square of paper.

Bishop held it close, turning it away from the wharf and the shadows, trying to catch the water-light.

He said: "I can't see it clearly here. Let me keep it, until we get somewhere brighter."

"All right. Don't lose it." A queer, dry tone grated out the next words. "And, Bishop, if you take it away from me altogether, I'll kill you, if I can. I want that man."

Bishop put the sketch into his pocket.

"We won't talk about killing," he said.

"You're not used to it. But I've talked about killing, and heard about killing, for a long time. I've been a murderer longer than I've been a man. They've all said so, haven't they? All of them—"

"Shut up."

Speight finished the last sandwich. The paper dropped to the ground. Bishop said quietly:

"You've told me all I wanted to know. But I must tell you something. Your wife doesn't think that anyone but you killed the girl. If the man who killed the girl has made himself a friend of Thelma's, she still doesn't realize who he is. Do you understand that?"

There was little feeling in his tone.

"Is it true?"

"I know that it's true."

"All right. I understand."

Bishop eased his legs straight, opening up from his crouching posture. He looked down at Speight.

"Tonight, you might meet your wife unexpectedly. If you do, remember what I've just told you. She's afraid of what you'll do to her."

The words had a metallic bitterness in them.

"I'm not interested in my wife. I don't want to do anything to her."

"All right. We'll go now."

The thin laths of the box creaked as Speight got off it. He said: "I'm too cramped for running."

"We may not have to run. Move about before we go."

Bishop watched him carefully as he flexed his legs, relieving the stiffened muscles. Bishop said:

"Feel all right?"

"I'm all right. I've eaten. A bit of bread can turn a mouse back into a man. And a bit of help can do the same." He looked at Bishop in the gloom. "I don't know what you get out of this. It must be a lot. For some queer reason I'm valuable to you. Otherwise you'd just drop me into the river."

Bishop said quietly: "You don't trust anyone at all, do you?"

"I don't even trust myself."

Bishop turned away.

"We'll go now. Do all I say. If we lose each other and you stay free, ring me again when you can. Someone'll be there."

He stopped at the corner of a wharf and looked behind him. Speight was hanging back.

"Come on, Speight."

Speight said softly: "There's quite a mob to get through. Isn't there?"

"Yes. But that's all right."

"I wish I could understand, Bishop. If you're caught with me, you're in trouble. Isn't that so?"

"That's so."

"Well—"

"Speight, we haven't got time. If it suited me better, I'd just drop you in the river. Remember?"

Speight moved, joining him at the corner of the wharf.

Bishop waited for a moment, listening, watching the skyline. The half-hour chime came down from Big Ben in a sequence of solid gold; then the echoes died across the Thames and the roofs and the streets.

Behind them the ripples lapped, slapping at the timber and the concrete wall. Above them the cranes leaned like empty gibbets. In front of them lay London, and the hunt.

Bishop moved forward.

20th

MOVE

♛ "YOU LOOKED edgy, at the Lotus Bowl."

"Did I?" She cupped her brandy glass, looking into it.

Willison said: "Obviously it's not my business."

"Oh, it's all right, Rex." Her head felt muzzy. "Someone I was expecting there didn't turn up, that's all."

He watched her, conscious that he was himself being watched by the long-featured brunette at the next table, conscious that his particularly blaze-blue eyes and magnificent shoulders always caught more than passing attention from women in restaurants. But just now Thelma was with him. There weren't many women like Thelma to look at, to be with, to touch. It was a shame she was so wrapped up in the Tasman boy; or maybe that was part of her attraction to others. He said:

"Would they have dined you, darling?"

In the clear round glass she saw reflections. One was Rex's face, round and brown and very white-teethed.

"They might."

"I'm glad they didn't show up."

She looked at him, her lids lifting slowly.

"It wouldn't necessarily have cut you out. I like you."

He gave a golden smile.

"I've always wanted a kid sister."

She smiled back. "Poor Rex. When a woman doesn't want you for your lean brown frame and the grin that goes with it, you just get lost in the forest, don't you?"

He grinned. He said: "Fashion talk."

"And you'd rather have passion talk."

She finished the brandy. He said nothing.

She added: "But don't let me be nasty. You've told me three new stories at the party, and all of them clean, and you've given me a marvelous dinner, and you haven't mentioned the word bed for two hours. And even then you were talking about the tax on mattresses." She touched his hand affectionately. "Willison has depths. Or heights."

He went on smiling. Thelma looked beautiful tonight. Since the third drink at the Lotus Bowl the strain had left her face, and she'd been almost happy. He knew that the thing that scared her would come back to her mind once the liquor wore off. But just now she was almost happy, and very good to look at.

He really began trying now.

"Just because I've asked you to the flat," he said easily, "it doesn't mean I'm vote-catching with good intentions. You told me that for some reason you were dreading the night—"

"I said that?" Her eyes grew wide.

"You did, darling."

"When?"

"At the Bowl."

For moments she didn't answer. He said:

"So I said why not have a meal and come along to help me sort out my pictures. That's not quite the same as a lawyer asking you to come and look over his quaint old deeds."

Her face relaxed. Rex was cosy to be with. He always left things light.

She said: "All right, I'll come. And thanks for asking me."

He settled the bill. They left the restaurant soon after nine o'clock. As she got into his American saloon she knew that this was a mistake. She knew that no one was really fooling her. She knew Rex.

He'd been drinking a little, too, without a scare to scare away with cocktails and Beaujolais.

Once in his flat, there might not be a chance of getting out, without slapping his face or calling for porterage.

If she were crystal sober she wouldn't be doing this. She wound down the window as they drove along, and closed her eyes against the draught of the slipstream.

After half a mile she opened her eyes and turned her head and said softly:

"Rex."

He looked at her.

"Rex, will you drop me at my flat, instead of yours?"

"Drop you?"

"Yes. Drop. I'm feeling tired. Too tired for sorting out pictures."

He didn't look annoyed. It was an effort.

She said: "I feel rather low-down, changing my mind. But I think I should. You're a nice person when you're being reasonable, but Willison the cave-man might take a bit of taming."

He drove on, turning across Leicester Square in the new direction, towards Thames Gardens.

"Some other time," he said.

She touched his arm.

"When you're reasonable you're really nice. Thank you for not even complaining."

He grinned.

"I never try something I don't think I can do. I don't think I could persuade you. I enjoyed the dinner. I'll settle for that."

They passed the Miller-Group building, down Fleet Street towards Ludgate Hill.

He said: "It's nice not to be working."

"Can you find someone else to play with, this evening?"

"Nobody as interesting as you. I'll just sort out my pictures."

The Packard stopped outside Thames Court, and Thelma got out.

"Thanks for a wonderful time, Rex."

"Good night, darling."

She went into the block of flats. The saloon moved off with its thirty-seven horse-power exhaust-surge. In the doorway across the road, Detective-constable Pratt did not move. It couldn't have been Speight in the Packard. And the woman had gone into the flats alone.

The woman sat on the bed. Ten minutes had gone by since Rex had dropped her; in ten minutes the secure feeling of his company had ebbed away. She wished she had gone to his flat.

The room was silent. The metal made a tiny clear sound as the bullets went into the chamber. She moved the catch to "safe," and sat holding the gun, weighing it as the thin bald man had weighed it in his hand.

She felt protected by the gun, yet also afraid of it. That she had bought it was a cold, hard confirmation of her fear. As a friend, it was ugly company.

Her hand opened. The gun lay on the bed. She went into the sitting-room, turning on the two other lamps. She checked the time. Since Rex had been with her, talking to her within touching distance, fifteen minutes had passed. And she was afraid again.

As last night, she was alone here in the flat. The realization drove her, this time, to action, instead of to morbid passivity. Going into the bathroom, she bathed her eyes, dabbing them with soaked cotton-wool. Her head was clearing, but her stomach was queasy. She took off her make-up, splashed her face in cold water, and made-up again carefully.

Then she telephoned Rex.

There was no reply.

She asked for Bristol, and was connected with Reception at Victor's hotel.

The voice was faint but clear.

"Mr. Tasman? Oh, he checked out this evening."

"You mean he took his luggage?"

"That's right. One moment, please, I'll make quite certain."

The wires became hollow threads. Waiting, she lit a cigarette. The girl came back.

"Yes, Mr. Tasman left at eight o'clock—just over an hour ago."

"Did—he say where he was going?"

"Why, no. But he re-booked his room for Monday."

"I see. Thank you."

She cradled the telephone, drew for a moment on the cigarette, and swung a glance towards the door leading to the bedroom. It was open, as she had left it, and the bedroom lights were still burning. The idea was stupid, but if she had to, she could reach the little gun in a few seconds.

She telephoned CAR 2330.

"This is Mrs. Tasman."

"Good evening, Mrs. Tasman."

"Is Mr. Bishop there?"

"No. I'm sorry, he isn't. This is Miss Gorringe. Can I help you?"

Ash fell from the cigarette. She looked down at the flower of gray flakes on the carpet.

"No, I—just wanted to talk to him. I missed him this evening at the Lotus Bowl."

"Oh, yes. He asked me to apologize for him, if you rang. Lady Verisham was detained. I understand Mr. Bishop will telephone you as soon as he comes in, and hopes to talk to you."

"I might not be here."

There was a slight pause. Then;

"I believe it's rather urgent that he contacts you this evening, Mrs. Tasman. Can you tell me where to find you, later?"

"I—I'm not sure where I'll be." Anywhere, with anyone. Not here, alone with the gun. "Can I ring again, when I know?"

"Please do. There'll be someone here."

"All right, Miss Gorringe. I'll do that."

"Thank you so much. You will remember that it's important, won't you?"

"Has anything happened?"

"No. Oh no, but they are the instructions Mr. Bishop left with me."

"Then I'll remember."

"Thank you. Good-bye."

Her hand lowered the receiver, resting on it as the line went dead. The plastic instrument was cool under her hand, for her hand was cold. The plaited wire flex was knotted in loops. It hadn't been untwisted for weeks. Victor had often said they must get one of those wire gadgets that kept the flex tidy.

Ash fell again from the cigarette, like a taper marking off the minutes. It was nine-twenty.

She left the telephone, fetched her stole and gloves, and looked round the room. The tiger-striped suite was like a group of barred windows, such as they had at asylums. The limed-oak draghtsman's desk, tidied yesterday morning by Victor, reminded her that he had left the hotel, but had not said where he was going.

She opened the door, taking one step into the passage.

Gun.

She came back quickly, going through into the bedroom. Almost she expected not to see it there, where she had left it on the bed. But it was there. Of course it was there.

As she picked it up, a sound reached her ears. She paused, thinking it strange that she could hear so clearly the sound of the lift-gates at the other end of the passage. Then she remembered that she had left the front door open when she had hurried back for the gun. The bedroom door was still open, too. That was how she could hear so clearly the sound of the lift-gates at the other end of the passage.

And the quiet footsteps.

The metal was cold in her hand. She stilled her breathing. The safety-catch moved to her touch.

Someone had come up in the lift; now they were walking along the passage, this way. One of the people who lived in another flat, perhaps next to this one. Just coming home.

But if she were really frightened, she must go into the sitting-room, and close the door, and lock it. Then it would be all right. She moved her feet; her legs were stiff, suddenly. They took her halfway across the sitting-room. She paused. The footsteps were louder; a man's, not hurrying, just coming slowly along.

She managed to reach the light switch and it snapped up cleanly. She should close the door, but if it were . . . if it were not just someone from the adjoining flats, she'd see him and something would happen to her, inside her. Just the sight of Mervyn walking towards her in the passage would break something delicate in her brain.

She must not see him. Let him come, let him kill her, but not . . . the sight of his face, his hands, his mad eyes—

She moved back slowly. Her left hand touched the arm of the settee and in a moment her shoulder met the door-post. She moved back, into the bedroom where the lamps were burning. When she felt the edge of the bed behind her she stopped.

She could move to her left or to her right; or she could look away, close her eyes. She could have closed the door as she had come into this room. But from the moment when she had begun to grope backwards from the other room, she had not moved her eyes from the gap of the open front door. If she saw him she would be shocked as mad as he.

Yet, even knowing this, she could not break her stare. Already she must be mad, watching the gap of the doorway. Because the footsteps were close now and he was coming in.

In the passage the faint pilot lights burned. The gap of the doorway was a parallelogram of soft light. The sitting room was dark. In here the lamps were brilliant. They gleamed on the little cold gun.

She stopped breathing.

The sound of his feet was near. The measure of his pacing slowed at the door. In the oblong gap she saw his silhouette, heard his voice:

"Thelma—"

Her head was flooded with the fierce final rush of the panic, but she heard faintly the *thok-thok-thok* of the thing that pulsed in her hand.

21st

MOVE

AFTER TWO hours, they had got through the worst of it. Speight said: "I'm beat."

He was a man to mean it. He was not easily beat. Bishop said:

"Just relax. It's roses all the way from now on."

He started the engine. The Rolls-Royce had been parked less than a quarter-mile from where he had met Speight. It had taken them two hours to reach it. From Chelsea Creek to Hungerford Bridge there was a fleet of Q-cars, patrol saloons and police motor-cycles. On foot there were double the constables at the beats; specials patrolled on a roving brief; and the plain-clothes branch had been drafted in from stations as far north as Maida Vale.

On an east-west line from Fulham to the city was an observation wall of men with eyes. South of the river, another wall ran from Wandsworth to Bermondsey. On the water, police launches kept on the move, swinging in at scheduled rendezvous points to check reports.

Earlier today, Mervyn Speight had been seen twice near the Thames. Tonight they wanted him. It was an order.

He sat in the car, beside Bishop, drenched in sweat that his nerves had forced from the pores.

Bishop said:

"Try not to go to sleep. Look natural. We'll soon be home."

The wheels turned smoothly.

Between Grosvenor Road and Sloane Square, Bishop counted twelve plain-clothes men and four constables patrolling singly. The gray Rolls-Royce passed two Humber radio saloons and a greengrocer's van that had never carried a carrot since it was built.

Speight murmured: "How long?"

His lids were made of lead.

Bishop said: "Not long. Five minutes."

Turning off Sloane Square he saw another patrol-car, and recognized Detective-Inspector Frisnay, standing beside it.

He sent the Rolls-Royce another thirty yards, slowing softly, then he pulled in to the curb. He said:

"It's all right. Just going to stretch my legs."

Speight did not move, did not answer. He sat propped like a dead man.

Bishop got out and walked back. The rear window of his car was very small and discreet as was fashionable in 1920. From where Frisnay was standing he couldn't see anyone in the car; but he might have seen Bishop's passenger as the car had driven past. If Frisnay wanted to blow the whole thing wide open at this particular moment Bishop wanted to know about it. He might be able to throw a damper on, in time.

Frisnay watched him coming up.

"Good evening, Freddie."

Frisnay screwed up his eyes at him. He was tired on his feet.

"D'you know anything?" he asked metallically. Bishop was a faint hope at times like this. He seemed to mooch round the place with his hands in his pockets and his damned old pipe going and pick on just the thing that half the Yard was scouting the town for. He was luck-prone, even in the middle of making himself a first-class nuisance.

Bishop said:

"Yes, old boy. I've got Speight in the car with me. D'you want him?"

Frisnay pursed his mouth. He was hellish tired. He grunted: "Don't worry, we'll get him. We can't fail. You know how many men we've laid on tonight?" He shook his head. "I can't even tell you. It's an official top secret. But it'd surprise you."

Bishop filled his meerschaum.

He said: "You're such a tease."

He struck a match. "Freddie, I'm throwing a party, later tonight. Informal little spree, at the Rothbury Club."

Frisnay moved out of the smoke cloud that was coming from the meerschaum. He said:

"I hope you have a nice gay time. Think of me, your ratepaid guardian of the night."

"You should come along," Bishop said. He dropped the match-stalk. "Look in about midnight."

"Yes," Frisnay said. "I'll wear my lavender chiffon. The one with sequins."

Inside the patrol car the radio began sounding. Frisnay turned his head to listen. It was a routine report, Bishop said:

"By midnight, Freddie, I think Speight should be there. So you can come officially. Bring all the boys. Drinks on me."

He turned away. His tobacco was burning satisfactorily and he'd said all he wanted to say.

Frisnay walked a few paces with him, watching his face. He said:

"Is this straight, Hugo?"

"Of course. You know me. Honest Joe."

Frisnay said nothing.

"Now I must cut, Freddie. I've got someone with me. See you about twelve."

He walked quickly to the Rolls-Royce. Frisnay had wanted to stroll with him. That would have been tricky.

He started the engine and grated the gears. Once the wheels were rolling he felt better.

Speight said with a dry voice:

"How long?"

"One minute. Just one more minute. Then you can sleep."

The gray saloon moved quietly down King's Road and, after a minute, turned into a mews.

Bishop cut the engine and looked sideways.

"All right," he said. "We're through."

22nd

MOVE

♛ WILLISON PRESSED his back to the wall of the passage. The powder compact had dropped on to the carpet.

After the quick triple report the silence was strange, and tensioned. In it he now heard her body slumping to the floor of the bedroom. He picked up the compact, went into the sitting room and closed the door. He switched the lights on.

He found Thelma in the bedroom, crumpled on the carpet. There was the smell of cordite.

He lifted her and laid her on the bed, feeling for the heartbeat, checking her pupils. It was just a faint.

He picked up the gun and put it into his pocket as he heard a door opening into the passage, and voices. He went into the sitting room. Someone tapped on the front door. He went and opened it.

A small, busy-looking little man started back with a nervous blink.

"What's happened?" he asked, almost indignantly.

"Happened?" Willison frowned.

"We heard shots." The little man span round to his wife, who was hovering in the doorway of their flat. "Didn't we, Mary?"

She nodded, speechless.

Willison said: "Oh, that." He grinned. The little man's wife looked at him. Some of her consternation receded. She thought, what a charming young man. "That wasn't shooting," he said. "The ice tray was jammed in the fridge. I was breaking it free."

This seemed to surprise them as much as the shots had. They made heavy weather of twisting their thoughts suddenly from belching flame and singing lead to an ice tray being unjammed by banging it with a tin-opener.

"Oh," the little man said. He turned to his wife, to see if she agreed.

Another door had opened and a stout man looked along the passage at Willison and called:

"Everybody all right?"

Willison said: "Yes, thanks, old boy."

"Good." The stout man slammed his door. You knew where you were with him.

A third man was coming along the passage from the stairhead, next to the lift. He was breathing hard as if he'd sped up the stairs instead of waiting about for the lift.

"What's up?" he asked Willison. Obviously it was no good asking the other man. He didn't look as if he'd ever know anything.

"Breach of the peace," Willison grinned. "I was unjamming an ice tray with a hammer. I didn't know I was waking the dead. I'm sorry."

The new-comer nodded, and turned back to the stairs.

"It's all right," he said. He thought he'd better get back to his post. But he'd had to leave it, in spite of orders. It had sounded like faint shots, from down in the street. Trust his luck. If only it could have been the Tasman woman shooting at Speight in defense or something, it would have clinched his promotion.

He went back into the doorway, opposite.

The little man in the passage looked at Willison again, and then hurried home, jostling his wife into the flat as if he had to shield her gaze from the hideous carnage of battered ice trays. He would always protect Mary from the sensational. She had bad nerves.

Willison went into the sitting room of the Tasman flat, and closed the door again, this time locking it. He could feel the warmth of the gun in his pocket against his thigh. It was lucky no one in the passage had noticed the two slugs that had gone into the door post. He didn't know where the third had gone after it had sung past his ear. All he cared was that it had gone.

He went back into the main bedroom, looked at Thelma, and fetched cold water, stinging her face with it. Then he found some brandy in the sitting room cabinet. In five minutes she came round.

She didn't realize what had happened. She jerked up on to her elbows, on the bed.

"Rex, he came in—he was here . . . "

He touched her gently.

"No, darling, he didn't, and he wasn't."

Her eyes were frightened still.

"I heard him—along the passage—didn't you see him?"

He sat on the edge of the bed. He said:

"Listen, honey. That was me, coming along the passage. Mervyn just wasn't in the picture. You've had the heebies about him since he got free, but this is serious." He tapped his pocket. "I didn't imagine you were gunning for him."

She closed her eyes for a while, trying to straighten things out. The brandy was good for her. After a time she opened her eyes and looked at Rex Willison.

"I didn't hit you?"

"Now you're really conscious." He gave a faint replica of his classic grin. "No, you didn't hit me. That wasn't your fault. I happened to duck when the first one missed my arm and warned me off."

"I'm sorry."

"That's all right. We've all got our funny little habits. But I'll keep the gun. D'you mind?"

She didn't seem to be interested in the gun.

"What did you come here for?"

He dropped her compact on the bed.

"You left it in the car."

She smiled weakly.

"It made a good excuse. Did you actually rifle my bag for it?"

He shook his head.

"No, you really left it. On the floor. But the next time you do it, I think I'll just turn it back by registered post. It'd be safer."

She was hardly listening. She stared at him, puzzled.

"Rex, there's something I've got to ask you. It's silly, but I can't think what it is. My head's all over the place—"

"Take it slowly. Relax—"

"I know what it was. You just said I've been scared about—Mervyn." She went on looking at him in silence.

He got off the edge of the bed, taking away the cold-water sponge and the brandy glass. Coming back from the kitchenette, he said: "I was working free-lance, two years ago. I covered most of the Joanna Martin murder, and some of the trial. I recognized you when you joined Miller-Group."

He gave her a cigarette and took one for himself, and lit both. He didn't look straight at her very much. She asked him quietly:

"You've always known I'm his wife?"

He nodded. "Yes."

"Have you—told anyone?"

He looked at her very straight and said:

"Yep. I've been trading the information for a guinea an inch to *Criterion*—"

"Sorry, Rex," she cut in quickly. "Sorry." She left the bed and fixed her make-up at the dressing-table. "You mustn't mind me. I'm not really conscious yet."

He tried a faint grin.

"That's all right."

"Does Maurice know you covered the trial?"

"Yes, I think so. He knows I recognized you. We just don't talk about it. Why should we? I'd say there are quite a few people who've recognized you since you got back from abroad. It seems more important to you than to us. Forget it."

She put some Guerlain behind her ears; the bottle banged sharply on the glass top of the dressing table. Her hands were not steady yet.

He was watching her in one of the mirrors, standing behind her near the bed, smoking his cigarette. There was no expression on his face. She turned.

"I wished I'd gone on to your place," she said. "I tried to phone you, but there wasn't any answer."

He said: "With your nerves in this mood, you won't want to stay here. I'll drop you anywhere you say. I mean drop you. No strings."

She looked round for her gloves.

"That's so nice that you think I might even relent and help you sort out your pictures. All right, I will, if you still want me to."

He put out his cigarette.

"Good." He followed her into the sitting room. She turned, touching his elbow.

"But, Rex—just the pictures, and coffee or something. Please."

He smiled.

"Of course. This isn't your night out. I don't want to add to the unpleasantness."

"It wouldn't be unpleasant." She moved past him, collecting her bag. "It's just that I rather like Victor."

She went to the front door. "I'm not coming back here tonight. I'll put up at Lake's Hotel if there's a room. Or somewhere."

"I'll help you find a room."

"Bless you."

She opened the door.

The telephone began ringing and she stared, swinging round.

"Would you answer it, please?"

He crossed the room, picking up the receiver.

"Hello?"

She waited by the door. She heard him say:

"Yes, just a minute."

He looked at her, holding out the receiver.

She said: "For me?"

"It's your number."

She went over to him.

"I thought it might be for Victor." She hesitated. "Did they say who they were?"

"No. It's a man. Voice is familiar, but I can't place it." He unblocked the mouthpiece and gave her the phone.

"Mrs. Tasman here."

Yes, his voice was familiar.

"Hugo Bishop. I'm sorry I wasn't in when you phoned."

"It wasn't very important. Do you still want to know where to find me when I—"

"No, Thelma. But I'd like to ask you along to a party."

"Whose?"

"Mine."

"How nice. Where?"

"The Rothbury Club."

"In Cardew Street?"

"That's right. No one will be there much until about twelve. Was that Rex Willison who answered just now?"

"Yes."

"I asked because I've been trying to phone him. I thought he might like to come along too."

She lowered the receiver.

"Hugo Bishop's got a party tonight. He says would you like to go."

Willison said: "Nice of him. Are you going?"

"Yes."

"Let me take you on from my place, then."

She said to Bishop: "Yes, we'd both like to come. Are you celebrating anything special, Hugo?"

There was a slight pause. Then:

"I don't know yet. See you about half-past eleven or twelve."

"All right." She hesitated. "Hugo?"

"Yes?"

"Your voice sounds a bit—odd."

"I know. I'm eating a banana."

She smiled. Since she had taken the receiver from Rex her hands had become perfectly steady; and she realized it.

"I didn't mean that sort of odd."

"Not the banana sort?"

"No. But I won't persist. We'll be there about midnight. And thanks."

"It'll be nice to see you. Good-bye, Thelma."

"Good-bye, Hugo."

Leaving the telephone, she found Willison looking serious-minded. He said carefully:

"My nostrils are quivering. Notice?" He quivered them for her benefit.

"Why?"

"I dunno. I get taken out, taken in, shot at, and then asked to a party. By Bishop. No wonder his voice sounded odd."

She smiled, opening the front door again.

She said: "At least you're still alive."

He followed her out, closing the door and noting the splintered path on the lintel, where the third bullet had struck. He said:

"Yes, that's something."

When the telephone began ringing again they were in the lift, and neither heard it. It rang for just over one minute; and then it stopped, and the flat was quiet again.

23rd

MOVE

BISHOP MOVED P-Kt4, ignoring an opportunity of blocking the red Rook.

Miss Gorringe said:

"That's interesting."

"I hoped you'd think so."

She moved her Queen, heading off a threat to her King's Bishop and a double check.

He looked at the wall clock. Her eyes followed his. She said:

"Five more minutes?"

He nodded. "Yes. We'll give him black coffee and a cold shower."

He moved P-B5, protecting his only Knight.

Miss Gorringe sat back in her chair.

"Sorry, Hugo. I haven't your flair for playing a

good straight-forward game when there's a case blowing up under our seats."

He smiled, putting another match to his white-bowled pipe.

"The lady retires?"

"No, I'm not retiring," she said firmly. "I'm just asking for an adjournment."

"So it shall be. Don't knock the board flying before we get back to it."

The wall clock was at fifteen minutes past eleven. Speight, on Bishop's bed, had slept for an hour and a half. In a few minutes they must wake him.

"Hugo, suppose nothing comes off at this party?"

He got up from the chess table to walk about.

"If nothing comes off, Speight goes back to Broadmoor, and we've failed. I'd still go on trying to get at the truth, even so; but it's while he's loose that we've got the best chance."

"You think so?"

"All the time there's an alleged killer-lunatic at large, people are jumpy. Especially any people who know more about Joanna Martin's death than they ought to. Before Speight goes back, they might make one jump in the wrong direction." He laid his hand on the head of the Siamese, stroking it back and back and back until she purred with a slow, sensual rhythm "And that's where we shall be," he finished quietly.

Vera Gorringe left the chess board and moved

to the door. "So, really, we're just hoping for the best, is that right?"

His head tilted.

"You could say that. I believe I've asked our man to the party—our Person. I believe I've asked the right mixture of people to promote a useful explosion: once someone sees Speight among the guests. If I've got the ingredients wrong, then this evening will go down in my diary as the Night of the Damp Squib. If I've done right, and there's an explosion, I think it should prove we've really got something against the Person—prove to the police, which is the vital point."

Miss Gorringe opened the door, looking again to the wall clock. She said:

"Unless it was a sex-motive with Speight, or a brainstorm, nobody's thought of a reason why he should have strangled Martin. You think our Person will have a clear, cold motive?"

"One that we can discover, anyway. Either money, or blackmail, jealousy, revenge, fear—we haven't been able to pin anything like that on Speight. We'll have to pin one of them on the Person, and clinch things tonight if it's possible."

"You don't like to think of Speight going back to the asylum, do you, Hugo?"

He turned, looking at her down the long room.

He said quietly: "No, I don't. Because I don't think he belongs there." He looked away. "Better wake him."

She nodded.

"All right. The coffee's ready. Will you have some yourself?"

"Please."

She went out.

Walking slowly down the room, he passed the little round chess table, where the board was set out. The pieces were employed in a rather tricky middle game; but he remembered placing some of them on his desk only yesterday—thinking of them as the characters in this case that was then beginning: Queen, Rook, Knight, King, Pawn . . . and a little to one side, the white Bishop, wondering where to begin. Now he passed the table and walked on towards the door, wondering how this other game would end.

He went into the bedroom and woke Speight.

"Black coffee," he said briskly. "Cold shower, shave, set of clean clothes. All right?"

He hated waking the man like this, after an hour and a half of sleep. He could do with twelve more.

Speight said:

"All right, Bishop."

He got off the bed, clamping his hands to his face, clearing his head.

At ten minutes to midnight, Speight was ready to go. His frame was trying to break out of the too-slim dinner-jacket that had come out of Bishop's wardrobe, and the trousers were over-long.

"Sorry I don't keep your size," Bishop said. "But you'll pass. How d'you feel?"

"All right," Speight said. He was quiet in his movements as he got into the Silver Ghost with Miss Gorringe and Bishop. He seemed to be holding himself back from something he wanted badly to take.

Bishop said: "It shouldn't be difficult for you tonight. Don't have too much to drink: you'll want to be alert. If you see the man we want, don't talk to him. Just tell me, and we'll do the rest."

Speight was beside the driver. He looked through the windscreen, his eyes level, his hands unmoving on his knees. He said nothing. Bishop started the engine.

"All understood, Speight?"

The cylinders began their sixfold whisper, under the long gray bonnet.

Speight said quietly:

"Yes."

Bishop looked at his expression, decided that Speight had understood, and moved the Rolls-Royce out of the mews.

Speight looked ahead, his eyes level, his hands motionless on his knees, staring through the windscreen without expression. Even from the back of the car, Vera Gorringe noticed a tension about his outline that did not make her easy.

The tires sighed over the dry roads, towards Cardew Street, towards midnight. The side-lights flickered in reflection across windows and the cellulose of other cars. The soft rush of power streamed from the engine, scarcely disturbing the silence of the streets.

Speight sat still, and looked ahead of him, and said nothing.

24th

MOVE

―――― ♛ AS BIG Ben sounded midnight, the
―――― chimes were heard by the men who
walked singly or in pairs through Westminster,
the men who sat in the black saloons with
their radio antennae sprouting thinly from the
roofs, and the men who perched astride their
patrol machines at the curbsides, watching the
streets.

Synchronized with the machinery of the great
clock above Parliament were the watches worn
by the more distant men, strung between Fulham and the city, Chelsea Creek and Hungerford
Bridge, Wandsworth and Bermondsey.

A few of the police-launches heard the chimes,
tolling above the throb of their engines and the

soft churn of their screws. In Scotland Yard, the radio-panel was receiving calls at the steady rate of six per minute.

S-17: Wandsworth Common: nothing to report.

S-29: Lavander Hill: proceeding east to Cedars Road: nothing to report.

Mowbray: Battersea Park Road: joined P.C.s 135, 137: nothing to report.

N-15: Lupus Street: returning to Pimlico Road: halted lorry FMQ1436 and questioned: no report.

N-35: King's Road: proceeding west to Beaufort Street: nothing to report. Please locate N-47.

N-47: Old Church Street: no report. Rendezvous with N-35 not yet made.

No news of Speight from anywhere.

But it was a rough night for the cracksmen, the balcony boys, the hot-feet, the getters, the draggers, the rag-tag-and-bobtail flitting the midnight streets. Alf Webster slid past a corner and cussed the constable, the jemmy up his sleeve. Billy Dwight waited with a warm engine and a load of nylons, scared of starting-up, scared of sitting here in the lamplight, wishing he'd backed out. Two of the Elephant mob played dice till it was clear, cursing each other with their nerves stringy and their ears riddled with the sound of feet outside, the sound of engines, and wheels, and gears.

It was a rough night for the boys. All over town there were splits, busies, dicks, bogies, flatties, the hot lot and the heavy mob. You couldn't put your mug outside the door without getting a flashlamp on it. Even the river was hot.

In the ballrooms, night-clubs and late-supper rooms, no one was worried by the police hunt that was spread like a net over London. They danced, ate, drank, and were merry. Nobody cared.

In the Rothbury Club there were perhaps fifty people, jammed loosely between the snack counter, the two bars, and the tiny dais where the four Bell Boys sent swing pulsing from their instruments.

A few people were dancing on the ten square feet of maple near the dais. Others were perched at the snack counter or the bars; the rest sat at the little round tables, drinking and looking. Nearly all were talking; whatever else they were doing, they were talking, too.

This was Hugo Bishop's party. Nobody knew why he was giving it, but that wasn't important. It was a good party, and these days good parties weren't often come by. No one could afford them anymore. Or if they could, they didn't know how to make them go. Hugo could, and Hugo did. Good old Hugo. 'Nother drink.

Most of them here were friends of his. The thing they didn't know (because it wasn't important) was that he was throwing this party for a few select guests; and these guests scarcely knew him at all. One or two had never even met him. But this little show was for them, chiefly, and especially for one of them.

And even Bishop didn't know, for certain, who that one was.

People were still coming in at ten past twelve, Vera Gorringe, in her Lady Verisham *ensemble*, but appearing under her own colors, was devoting herself to the duties of hostess, leaving the host to go his elegant way among the guests on his special errands that they didn't know about. It just wasn't important. It was a wonderful party and everyone looked very happy. And there was Joan Deste, coming in now. Dear old Joan, looking marvelous. Must round up a gin for her.

A man was sitting alone, at a small table in the corner of the room. He had a drink in front of him. He was just sitting there and sipping his drink and looking at the people. The lighting was soft in here, and he sat almost in shadow. Nobody worried, nobody cared.

Bishop had reached the boyish-looking type near the main doors, the one whose hair wouldn't seem to stick down behind the crown. He looked as if he didn't use his dinner-jacket often. But he looked quite nice. Everybody here looked nice. Even old Barney was dancing, ten years younger on four Tom Collins, and falling for Marjorie, hook, line and doughnut.

Bishop said to the boyish-looking type:

"Come on and I'll get you another drink."

Freddie Frisnay nodded pleasantly.

"All right," he said.

Bishop led him through the pack, skirted the dance floor, piloted him past the longer bar and stopped by the little round table in the corner, looking down at Speight.

"Hello, Merton," Bishop said cheerfully. He put a hand on Frisnay's shoulder. "Merton Late— Freddie Frinton."

Speight nodded. Frisnay smiled nicely. Bishop led him onward, telling Speight: "Got to find this man a drink. He can still say the Leith police dismissed us. I'll come back."

Standing at the bar, Bishop handed Frisnay a drink, and said:

"Satisfied?"

Frisnay nodded.

"Yes. I'm damned if I know how you did it."

He sipped his drink. He added:

"You know I can't let him leave here. Don't you?"

"Of course. That's all right. But let him stay here until I've found what I want. Bargain?"

Frisnay brooded. Then he said:

"It's not going to be easy to persuade the Chief. I'll have to tell him who's here, and he'll want me to take him along right away."

"You owe it to me to persuade him. I've got your man, at a price. My price is a couple of hours, at the outside."

"I'll do my best."

As Frisnay began wandering toward the main doors, Bishop said:

"If the Chief isn't happy, ask him along here. Honored guest—if he comes incognito."

Frisnay nodded. He went out of the room. In the foyer was Sargent Baxter, an official guest, one hand in his pocket, a drink in the other. He had come out here for air. Officially.

"Baxter," Frisnay murmured, "he's in there."

Baxter's expression didn't change. It was the only one he had. But he said:

"Well, I'll go to hell, sir."

Frisnay nodded. He still couldn't understand how Bishop had done it, but it was no use worrying about it now. He said:

"Speight's at one of the tables by the wall. Across to the right, in the corner, sitting alone. I don't believe he knows our lot are here. Go in and wander about. Post Brickley on these doors. Hobson in the cloak-rooms, Jones on the other door near the long bar and Wilson can have a roving commission inside the building. All right?"

"Yes, sir. Anyone can leave?"

Frisnay nodded.

"Except Speight."

He went to the telephones, going into the end booth.

As the quarter chimed from Westminster, S17 and S-29 started up at Wandsworth Common and Lavender Hill and, with a dozen other patrol cars, headed back to their depots. The rest continued on their schedule, with changed orders.

N-15, N-35 and N-47 left Lupus Street, King's Road and Old Church Street and proceeded to the Yard. A motorcycle started up along the Embankment; a pair of plainclothes men turned away from the winking-light box in Cannon Street, and waited for the dark, blue van; a special turned to his mate on Vauxhall Bridge, walking down to the station, and said: "It look's like they've got him."

On the broad sweep of the river, the dark blue launches were turning towards their rendezvous points along the banks, signaled in by morse lamps. Their wake subsided across the water, and the throb of their engines died.

A closed van swung round from Leicester Square and pulled into the curb, alongside the man in the trilby.

"Hop in," the driver said.

He climbed aboard.

"Have they got him, then?"

"Must have, I s'pose."

The gears grated; the wheels moved; the van turned toward Coventry Street.

Over London, the hunt was coming home. The meshes of its net were falling away, strand after strand of it breaking as the minutes passed, as the radios spoke, as the orders changed.

All that remained by half-past midnight was a small ring of quiet men, enclosing the Rothbury Club, Cardew Street, W.1.

Most of them could hear the sounds of the

party that was going on three floors above street level. They looked upward, sometimes, to the bright windows; then their eyes returned to the doors of the building. Their orders were simply to wait.

Inside the building were other men. On the third floor, behind the bright windows, Sargent Baxter was dancing with a nice little thing in *broderie-anglaize* and Debrett; and at the bar, Rex Willison was saying to Maurice Jerrold:

"You know, it wouldn't be any good seeing ourselves as others see us." He looked round the crowded room, listening to the high drone of talk. "We simply wouldn't believe it."

Jerrold smiled, moving his glass clear of a passing elbow. He said: "Oh, well, everybody's happy. What's it matter what we look like?"

"It couldn't matter less," said Willison. He was cold sober after five straight gins. Later, he'd warm up.

The quartet went into its own quick version of *Broadway Beat*, and the floor was jammed in a minute.

At a table by the dais, Eve Jordan said to Thelma Tasman:

"Darling, I've no faintest clue. this person, Miss Gorringe, phoned me soon after seven, and said you'd rather like me to be here, and that it'd be a nice party. I tried to phone you—no luck—and just came up."

Thelma looked at the dancers, and saw Rex

steering a rather thin girl into the scrum. She said:

"I don't really know why I'm here myself. But I trust Hugo. He must have a good reason."

Eve said: "It's a good party. What else matters?"

Across the room were their host and a friend of his, Freddie Frinton. Bishop had given him a square of soiled paper.

Frisnay looked at it for a full minute. Then he said:

"Can I keep it?"

"For the time being."

Frisnay looked up from the portrait, his eyes touching on one face after another across the packed room, dismissing each. After a while he said without turning his head:

"The original's in here?"

Bishop said: "Yes." He was looking over to the tiny dance floor. "I think you'll recognize him easily. I did. See if we agree."

Frisnay moved his eyes, searching the faces.

"You believe," he said quietly, "quite off the record, of course, that this might be the picture of the man who killed Martin?"

"We shouldn't ignore the idea."

"Officially I have to, at this stage. If my Chief turns up, don't throw your idea into any discussion we have with him."

"I won't. I'm satisfied—at this stage—that I've put the idea to you. As long as it's inside your head, it'll give your own line a definite slant."

Frisnay said: "Leave it like that for now."

"Fair enough."

He left Frisnay and made his way to the dance floor. The band was using a guitar now, and one of the boys was singing a Flamenco tolerably well considering his English temperament.

Willison was coming off the floor with Helen Shelly, a tall girl with a winter-sports tan and a mouth as disturbing as a tantalus. He grinned happily at Bishop and said:

"When are you coming to see the photographs?"

Bishop said: "Photographs?"

"We were talking about them at the du Vancet show."

Bishop smiled, remembering. He said:

"I'll wait for Monday's editions."

Willison frowned.

"I don't sort of connect."

"They should be on the street on Monday. To remind the public. Old news never dies."

Willison said: "I wish you'd explain."

"I will. But not just now."

The tall girl said:

"Hugo, you've got the nicest people here."

She hung on his arm. She was just that degree happier than a glass of water would have allowed.

He said: "You asked me why I invited you. Now you know." He peeled her off him gently and handed her back to Willison.

"Have a good time, Helen."

She willowed away over the dance floor, humming to the band. Willison gave Bishop a final glance and was lost in the crowd.

Bishop watched him go, then moved slowly round the room, sitting down for a moment at one of the more secluded tables.

He asked:

"May I?"

"Hello, Mr. Bishop. I'm wonderful sloshed."

He smiled affectionately. This was one of his special guests, one of the reasons for the party that the others didn't know about. He said:

"You look wonderful, sloshed. But don't pass out. You'll miss the fun."

Her eyes were very bright and her dress was as cheap as her accent, but she looked happy, and people looked all right when they were happy. She said with a faint giggle: "You know, I'm not really conscious except when I'm like this."

Bishop looked up and intercepted one of the waiters. He changed her empty glass for a full one.

She looked at it lovingly.

"You're goin' to ask me to all your parties, aren't you, dear?"

He smiled and said yes, he was.

"All of them," she giggled dreamily. "Every bloody one."

He sent a slow wink across to Vera Gorringe, who was talking to Joan Deste. She cocked a gentle eyebrow. He answered with a slight shrug. It wasn't zero hour yet.

He said to the girl: "I don't even know your first name."

"Lizabeth," she said. "Lizabeth Martin."

He got up. He said gently, "Yes, I know your surname. But I like Elizabeth. I'll call you that."

"No, call me Liz."

But he had got lost in the crowd. He was an awfully nice feller. In the pub he'd seemed too serious, like. She'd even thought he was a dick, or one of them reporters. But now she knew he was a real gentleman, like Joanna used to pick up with, only this one was *real*. He didn't try mucking about, not in that way. He was awfully nice. She was awfully happy.

She picked up her gin.

The Bell Boys played *Sirocco,* with a hot, sweet rhythm and a muted horn. Someone had brought some balloons in, and people were throwing them up. It was only one o'clock, but the pressure was fierce.

Underneath one of the ornate wall lamps, Frisnay was standing alone, looking at one of the crowd. It was a man, and instantly recognizable. Speight was said to be a good artist. Frisnay thought he was. The portrait, despite the distortion of its evil expression, was acutely definitive. The original was certainly in this room.

Bishop passed him, talking to a man who looked like a successful uranium merchant. Bishop turned his head and murmured:

"Well?"

Frisnay said: "Yes. It's a good portrait."

Bishop walked on.

Frisnay went on looking absently at the man whose face had been sketched so accurately by the mad artist; and he wondered if this man could really have killed the girl on the bombed site, and not Speight. For Speight, this party was a kind of retrial of his innocence and sanity. He sat over there, alone at the little table, pronounced guilty and mad. Bishop had brought him here to face a new trial that the law couldn't have granted the man: because he had been tried once, convicted once, sentenced to Broadmoor for all time ... or until the Queen's pleasure was known.

People tilted their glasses, drinking and talking, dancing and laughing, moving among the soft lights and the gaudy beat of the musicking on the dais; and above them and among them floated the colored balloons that someone had brought along.

While Speight sat at the table, in the dock.

The music caught a swirl of people on the maple floor, swinging their limbs around and along, guiding into the maze.

Victor Tasman came in through the main doors.

Frisnay saw him one second later.

Sergeant Baxter looked across to Detective Constable Brickley.

Hugo Bishop broke off what he was saying to the uranium merchant when he saw the figure in the doors and recognized it as Tasman's.

Vera Gorringe left the group of people by the snack bar and crossed the width of the room, meeting Tasman.

She had been briefed.

"Victor Tasman, isn't it?"

He looked worried.

"Yes, I—"

"I'm Vera Gorringe, your hostess. So glad you managed to get here." She hog-tied a waiter, put a drink into Tasman's hand, and tucked her fingers lightly into the crook of his elbow. "Thelma's somewhere over there—let's find her."

Bishop turned back to his companion.

Frisnay looked down at his cigar.

Thelma left her table.

"Victor, darling!"

He smiled, breaking the worry on his face.

"Hello, sweetheart."

Vera Gorringe left them.

They sat at the small table. Eve Jordan said:

"Everybody's here. Simply everybody. Simply everybody. Even me, and now even you. How's your aeroplane factory?"

He said: "I got fed up with it." He looked at Thelma. Softly: "You all right?"

"Of course. I wish I'd known you were coming—"

It was all right to say things in front of Eve. He

said: "You sounded worried, on the phone last night."

"It—wasn't anything."

"Well, I planned to get an afternoon train up, and go back on Monday. Then business got frantic—the new blower's going rather well—and I had to hang on. But I had a phone call from Vera Gorringe—"

"Saying," Eve Jordan cut in, "that Thelma would rather like you to come and join her at this party."

He quizzed her.

"How did you know?"

"I just guessed."

She toyed with her drink, looking down at it. He looked at Thelma. "I tried to ring you when I got to town, but there was no answer." He touched her hand across the table. "It wasn't anything important last night?"

She shook her head.

"No, Victor. Nor tonight. None of us know why we're here, but our host's a friend of mine, Hugo Bishop—"

"Yes, his name was mentioned over the phone."

"You'll like him. I expect he's a bit tied up at the moment." She held his eyes for a moment. "I'm so happy you're here, darling."

He freed her hand.

"Shall we dance?"

She got up. He said to Eve: "Excuse us?"

"Have a good time."

They squeezed their way to the dance floor.

The band played their own futuristic version of *Bolero*, which brought it back almost to the classic original, though they didn't realize this.

Hugo Bishop was talking to Rex Willison, crossing the room slowly from the snack counter to the long bar, round the fringe of the crowd. When they were near the small table in the corner, Bishop sighted a late guest and left Willison to get himself another drink.

Bishop dealt with the late guest in fifteen seconds, crossed the room again and stood with his back to the wall. He looked toward the spot where he had left Willison.

Frisnay was looking in the same direction, from his position at the bar.

Sergeant Baxter was near the main doors, a few yards from Bishop.

One minute passed and *Bolero* gave way to something that Sinatra had bestowed upon the waiting world, and Bishop saw Willison coming.

He was moving deceptively quickly through the crowd toward the main doors. Frisnay didn't move. Bishop took a step forward.

"Not going, Willison?"

Willison's eyes were bright. He had been shocked sober.

"No. Just to use the phone."

Bishop didn't move.

He said: "Urgent?"

Willison nodded.

"A red-hot story for the street. Mervyn Speight's here. Is that what you meant when you talked about Monday's editions?"

"You've recognized Speight very easily. He's almost in the dark over there."

Willison set his face.

"I photographed him two years ago. I told you. I've seen his picture in today's papers. So has everyone." He controlled his voice. "I'd like to phone the story."

Bishop's expression was pleasant. A lot of people were here: he was their host; he was talking to a guest. He said softly:

"Willison, if you just want to phone the story, you can do it within an hour of now, and you'll have it exclusively. I can guarantee that."

Willison hesitated, facing him.

Detective-Inspector Frisnay watched him from the bar. Detective-Sergeant Baxter's head was turned, and he watched Willison's face in a wall-mirror by the doors. Vera Gorringe had stopped talking to Mabel Harvey, across the room, and her large colorless eyes were absorbed.

Willison said:

"I've just dug up a big story. I want to send it in. Do you object?"

Bishop said pleasantly: "No, but you'll be going off at halfcock. I could give you more than just Speight sitting there. Outside the building there's a cordon of fifty men. There are police in here, all nice and dressed up. The inspector in charge is watching you now. I could go on—but not if you go busting out and blowing the thing up half-cooked."

Willison's face was tensed. A jaw muscle was moving. His eyes never left Bishop's. He said after a moment:

"All right. But I get it exclusive?"

"You do."

"Then I'll play."

Bishop opened his cigarette case. Willison took a cigarette and lit it.

"Thanks," he said.

As he turned away, Bishop said cheerfully:

"Glad you're being sensible, Willison. You wouldn't have reached the telephones, anyway. There's a security black-out on."

Vera Gorringe turned to Mabel Harvey.

"I'm so sorry, my dear. I was day-dreaming. As I was saying, this concert is next Tuesday and I honestly believe it's going to be hard to get seats, so if you'd like a couple—"

Frisnay looked for somewhere to drop the ash from his cigar.

Sergeant Baxter thought he'd have a second drink, against orders. All the time Speight was here he'd be as sober as a police report, whatever he drank.

The foursome swung into *Bronx Jinx* to clear the floor and give the darlings a rest; because nobody here tackled jive.

Bishop met Thelma and Tasman leaving the floor. Tasman was looking less worried. Bishop introduced himself, apologized for being so busy, and took them back to Eve Jordan's table, working out a pattern of position and timing among his special guests that he and Frisnay had agreed on.

He said to Tasman: "Tell Eve about your new supercharger. She's been asking me."

Eve Jordan looked wide-eyed at Bishop. Tasman sat down. Bishop moved Thelma's chair for her, bending forward. He murmured:

"You can trust me absolutely. Everything is supremely organized and there's not a thing to worry about."

Her head was half-turned. She looked at the flowers on the table. He finished softly:

"Mervyn is here, having a good time." He sensed her quick shiver and put his hand on her arm. "So if you see him, don't worry. And don't recognize him."

She said nothing.

"Promise?" he asked gently.

She nodded, and after an instant said:

"Yes, Hugo."

Only when he excused himself to the others and walked away did she look round; but his back was turned to her.

The fourth Bell Boy sang:

"Come on roun—tew my-house, bebby—'s'nob-'dy-in-but-meee!" He repeated this.

There were now sixty or seventy people in here. Twelve balloons had burst, but someone had brought some more. A few people were sitting at tables because, frankly, they couldn't stand up. Why hadn't somebody *told* them what Hugo's parties were like?

Someone else had got hold of streamers, and Detective-Inspector Frisnay looked a little like a wedding. The dance floor was packed again and there was a little plump man jigging up and down on the top of a nearby table. The floor just wasn't big enough, and it was a good idea. Others were taking his lead. It looked a bit silly, but nobody cared.

The waiters were looking hot and creased. The bars were sticky. In the main crush there were three visible shoulderstraps, and one of Coast-National's leading starlets was looking for her shoe.

The trumpet squeaked with a fierce neurotic superblast. The percussion man went mad. The balloons went up. The streamers came down. This was just not in our world.

Rex Willison was standing, stiff-faced, at the end of the bar. Maurice Jerrold was between the main doors and the dais, his drink on a table. Thelma Tasman sat with Victor Tasman and Eve Jordan quite near him. Elizabeth Martin was three tables away, nearer the doors, talking to an R.A.

Frisnay had not moved. Sargent Baxter had

moved three yards, towards the doors. Vera Gorringe was alone, on the fringe of the main crowd and covered in streamers.

Bishop was stopping at Speight's table, in the shadowed corner. Speight had had one drink. The empty glass was in front of him.

He looked up.

Bishop smiled. He said above the blare of the band:

"Another five minutes, and we can take you to a bed, and you can finish your sleep."

Speight's eyes were almost blank. His voice was dull.

"I don't need sleep."

Bishop said:

"Then let's just stretch our legs."

Speight got up, like an automaton with the button pressed. He looked awkward in the borrowed dinner-jacket. He looked dead on his feet.

Bishop gave him a cigarette, lit it for him, and began walking with him along the edge of the crowd. A balloon popped just behind them.

The air was sticky with heat, with light, with sound.

The Bell Boy sang:

"*J'attendrai . . . le jour et la nuit . . . j'attendrai toujours . . . ton retour. . . .*"

Joan Deste was with Mabel Harvey, talking about Steiner's genius.

The Coast-National girl had found her shoe,

and lost her balance. A script writer was help
ing her.

An American model was draped all over a
young man with spectacles. He said defensively,
"Darling, you're tight."

She giggled seriously: "On the con-trary, darling, I'm loose."

"*J'attendrai . . . car l'oiseau qui s'en fuit . . .
vient cher-cher l'oubli . . . dans son nid. . . .*"

A girl near the doors lost the thread of what
her friend was saying because something had
distracted her. She said:

"But look."

Her friend turned, slopping her drink.

A big man was standing by a table. His face
was alabaster white. Next to him was a slim man
with light-colored hair and grey eyes. Near them
was a middle-aged society dame in a wonderful
black gown.

Facing the big white-faced man was a man
almost as big, but wearing the oddest clothes
that were just busting at the seams. In his hand
was a gun.

The girl near the doors said:

"What in a blue moon's happening?"

Her friend said with a loose mouth: "I just
haven't a clue."

Others had noticed, had stopped talking,
stopped drinking, stopped moving. A pool of silence had formed at this side of the room; and it

was spreading, creeping among the crowd, until at last the only sound was the pulsing beat of the band.

Inspector Frisnay jerked a nod to Brickley. Brickley moved toward the dais. In a moment the music faded, as if under a damp blanket.

Frisnay said clearly:

"Speight."

Speight did not turn his head, did not move his eyes. His eyes were fixed on Jerrold. Jerrold stood with his hands hanging, sweat beading on the white of his face. He stared Speight back.

Frisnay said:

"Speight. Don't do anything. It's all right."

Bishop, standing near Jerrold, sent a glance at Frisnay. Frisnay thought Speight ought to be humored, thought Speight was insane. It might be that he was right.

Thelma and Eve and Tasman were on their feet, watching from a few tables away. Thelma was pale.

Near Bishop, Vera Gorringe murmured:

"Hugo, did you know he'd brought a gun?"

Bishop's throat was tight.

"No."

Rex Willison was halfway between the long bar and the doors. His eyes were intent.

Speight stood without moving a muscle. Three blue streamers were coiled over his shoulders; the end of one of them hung down over his gun-wrist. His finger was inside the trigger guard. The catch was off.

The distance of Jerrold from Speight was some seven or eight feet. The gun was trained on Jerrold's stomach.

Frisnay said:

"We'll see to him for you, Speight. You leave him to us."

Silence came again.

Speight said in a low, steady tone:

"I've made so many pictures of you. Now I'm looking at you. After two years."

A girl on the dance floor began being softly hysterical just because she didn't understand what was happening or why the man wanted to shoot the other man. Somebody made her be quiet.

Speight said: "You've got a few seconds more. To me they're beautiful. It's like breaking the surface and seeing the sunlight—"

Frisnay said: "Speight, listen to—"

"And the sunlight's blinding and wonderful. And you're going under next, down in the dark."

Jerrold could not move his eyes. He looked white, and empty, and old. He did not even look afraid.

Bishop slowly folded his arms, slowly across his stomach. He was quietly furious with Speight. A bullet would smash everything.

He began moving, as he began talking. He

moved incredibly slowly, doing his best to balance his feet, sliding them an inch at a time over the carpet.

"Speight, you're letting me down badly. I was a damned fool to trust you. I suppose I don't care very much now you've taken this line. But I'm sorry you want to go back."

On the dais the drummer let a stick fall by accident. Some of the women drew their breath at the alien sound. One was crying, her face buried against a man's chest. She was young, and she had only read about things like this. She didn't want to see them.

"I'm sorry you want to go back."

His feet moved another inch, in a kind of slow-motion Charleston over the carpet.

"I've done the hell of a lot, you know, to stop you going back. Now you're just being a plain fool. You're going to shoot this man, and then you're going to be taken back to all those walls, and the trees—nothing but trees. Remember?"

Speight's expression altered, so slightly that the change was scarcely visible. Bishop was in a queer way tuned-in to that bruised mind; and he understood why Speight wasn't going back. He was going to shoot this man, but he wasn't going back.

Bishop's feet were moving. His body half-covered Jerrold's in the gun's line.

"All right, so you'll use the second bullet on yourself. Just when I can fix things so that you can stay free for always, you want to kill yourself. Is that sense?"

Vera Gorringe was watching Speight. She could not look at Hugo. There was nothing she could do. He was as mad as Speight, as this mad, suicidal party.

Behind Speight, one of the guests had begun to move, as quietly and as slowly as Bishop was moving now. Bishop said:

"Listen, and try to take this in. If you put that gun down now, you needn't die, and you needn't go back. Because we know now that you don't belong there. You're not insane. You're trying to be a first-class fool."

He stopped moving. His body covered Jerrold's. Speight was staring at him as though hypnotized by his voice, by the sudden bewilderment of seeing him there, in front of the other man.

In the crowd of people a man began babbling. He had emerged from a ten-brandy bender to find a scene he couldn't understand.

Bishop called clearly: "If everyone keeps quiet, It'll be a great help."

He lowered his voice.

"Speight, if you shoot now you'll kill me. All I've tried to do is to help you. If you shoot now you'll prove yourself insane."

A silence came, so deep that Jerrold's breathing was all that brought imperfection.

Vera Gorringe had turned her head and was

looking at Hugo. Her lips moved; her mind groped for the right words; but she said nothing. If Hugo got through this, he'd never forgive her for breaking down.

The air was sticky with the heat, the light and the silence. Seventy people stood in a nightmare, and no one spoke.

The man behind Speight was near enough now, and as he brought his clenched hand down on Speight's gun-wrist, the breath jerked audibly in his throat a fifth-second before the hammer struck the case and sent the bullet ploughing into the carpet.

Speight cried out and Frisnay made a dive from the doorway with Baxter beside him. The gun's explosion had battered the silence and seventy human nerve systems had reacted to the shock. A lot of women were hysterical; the rest were too absorbed in the struggle that Speight was putting up against the half-dozen men who were straining to hold him.

The gun had jerked across the floor and had hit someone's foot. Someone else picked it up and held it stupidly, wondering what to do with it. The acrid smell of cordite was in the air.

Frisnay said: "All right, get him outside."

Speight had stopped struggling. Everything in him had snapped, because sleep was crowding his nerves, adamant at last.

They got him into the foyer, through the main doors. Bishop went with them, his arm linked

with Maurice Jerrold's. One of Frisnay's men
was leading a girl out—Elizabeth Martin.

Vera Gorringe reached the doors and turned,
giving a signal to the band. The band began
playing, raggedly at first. She went out. The
doors were closed behind her.

In the foyer, Bishop said to Elizabeth Martin:

"Do you know this man, Liz?"

Her eyes were very wide and blue, and her face
was flushed. She'd been jerked out of her gin
session so fast that she was fully conscious even
though sober. She looked at Jerrold. She said:

"I've seen him before, yes."

Frisnay said: "When?"

She looked at him pertly.

"You a reporter?"

Frisnay said:

"Police. When?"

"P'lice, eh? Couple of years ago. He was one of
Joanna's men."

"You remember his name?"

Bishop looked at Frisnay. Elizabeth looked at
Jerrold. She said: "No. We called him The Gent."

Sergeant Baxter was using shorthand. Vera
Gorringe looked across at Mervyn Speight. He
was sitting on a gold-colored chair, his head in
his hands, with three or four men standing by.
But he was a limp, exhausted body and nothing
more, with sleep almost knocking it down.

Jerrold said in a queer, drained voice:

"In a way, I'm so glad. You don't know what it's

been like, thinking about him. For two years. But my wife—"

Frisnay warned him formally. He then asked;

"Did you kill Joanna Martin, on the bombed-site in—"

"Yes," Jerrold said, "yes . . . yes . . . yes."

Frisnay asked;

"Why did you do it?"

Jerrold's voice was almost level. It sounded as if he were talking about someone else instead of himself.

"I got involved with Joanna Martin about three of four years ago. It happened—after an all-night party. I had to pay her off." His head was slightly bowed. His hands were together and held in front of him. He looked down at them. "Two years ago she saw me again, and she made certain demands."

His tone began faltering, and lost its level monotony. It became higher, in defense. "I had a reputation . . . a family. Why should a woman like that smash up a—"

"I think," Frisnay cut in brusquely, "we'll go to the station now. You can make a full statement there."

Jerrold said nothing more. He didn't look away from his hands. These were the hands that had brought him to this midnight, and no others.

Frisnay nodded to Sergeant Baxter. Bishop went over and looked down at Speight. He said softly:

"It's all right, Speight. You didn't escape for

nothing. It doesn't look as if you must go back."

Speight did not move.

One of the men with him said:

"I think he's out."

Bishop nodded. He looked across at Frisnay.

"He can do with twelve hours' sleep."

Frisnay began moving Jerrold, with two of his men. He said:

"He'll have it. Can we meet tomorrow?"

"Yes. Not before noon. I'm a bit jaded myself."

He went back into the long room with Vera Gorringe. He knew something of how Speight felt. Since yesterday morning, nobody concerned with this business had slept much.

The band was still playing, and a few people were dancing. The nightmare seemed to be over. In here, with the lights and the music, had it ever begun?

Someone said to Bishop:

"Your parties always go with a bang, Hugo."

He gave a faint smile.

"Thanks. But not always by design."

Rex Willison was waiting near the doors. He came up. Bishop said:

"Go and phone your scoop. But don't say Speight was run to earth at my party. Say it was his own. I threw it for him."

When Willison had gone, Bishop turned to Vera Gorringe, glancing toward the dance floor.

He said:

"May I have the pleasure, Lady Verisham?"

Adam Hall is the pseudonym of Elleston Trevor, the author of over 20 novels. Mr. Trevor resides in Cave Creek, Arizona.

THE CLOCKS

Hercule Poirot has a problem—four clocks, all set to 4:13 were left at the scene of a murder. Poirot must solve this case in time before another murder occurs. (0-06-100279-8)

CAT AMONG THE PIGEONS

Summer school has just started at the exclusive Meadowbank school. In the middle of the night, the gym mistress is murdered... (0-06-100284-4)

THE SEVEN DIALS MYSTERY

A country house guest is found dead from an overdose of sleeping medication. On the mantel, seven clocks are lined up, all ticking ominously. The clues lead to the mysterious Seven Dials Society. (0-06-100275-5)

THE MURDER OF ROGER ACKROYD

No one is sure if Mrs. Ferrars poisoned her husband. Then there is another victim in a chain of death. Follow master detective Hercule Poirot as he takes over the investigation. (0-06-100286-0)